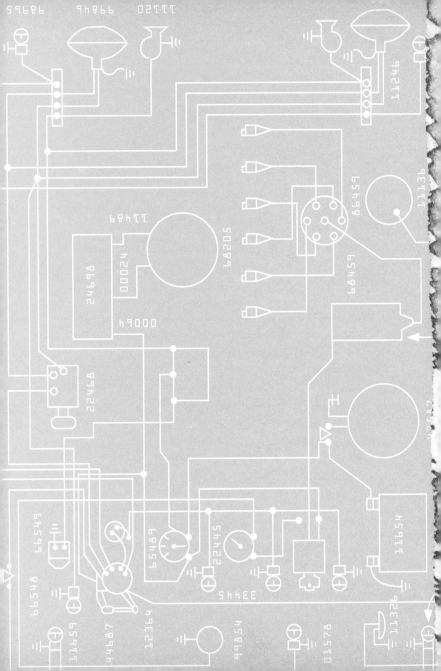

NICK AND TESLA'S

SUPER-CYBORG
GADGET GLOVE

!

A MYSTERY WITH

A BLINKING, BEEPING,
VOICE-RECORDING GADGET GLOVE
YOU CAN BUILD YOURSELF

QUIRK BOOKS
PHILADELPHIA

BY "SCIENCE BOB"
PFLUGFELDER AND
STEVE HOCKENSMITH

ILLUSTRATIONS BY
SCOTT GARRETT

Copyright © 2014 by Quirk Productions, Inc.

All rights reserved. No part of this book may be reproduced in any form without written permission from the publisher.

Library of Congress Cataloging in Publication Number: 2013956139

ISBN: 978-1-59474-729-8

Printed in China
Typeset in Caecilia, Futura, and Russell Square

Designed by Gregg Kulick, based on a design by Doogie Horner
Illustrations by Scott Garrett
Production management by John J. McGurk

Quirk Books
215 Church Street
Philadelphia, PA 19106
quirkbooks.com

10 9 8 7 6 5 4 3 2 1

DANGER! DANGER!

Before you build any of the projects in this book, ASK AN ADULT TO REVIEW THE INSTRUCTIONS. You'll probably need their help with one or two of the steps, anyway. While we believe these projects can be safe and family-friendly, accidents can happen in any situation, and we cannot guarantee your safety. THE AUTHORS AND PUBLISHER DISCLAIM ANY LIABILITY FROM ANY HARM OR INJURY THAT MAY RESULT FROM THE USE, PROPER OR IMPROPER, OF THE INFORMATION CONTAINED IN THIS BOOK. Remember, the instructions in this book are not meant to be a substitute for your good judgment and common sense.

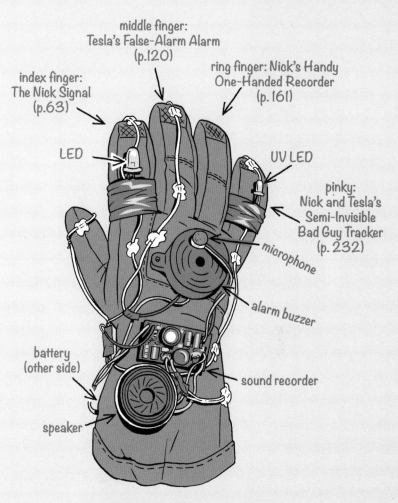

index finger:
The Nick Signal
(p.63)

middle finger:
Tesla's False-Alarm Alarm
(p.120)

ring finger: Nick's Handy
One-Handed Recorder
(p. 161)

LED

UV LED

pinky:
Nick and Tesla's
Semi-Invisible
Bad Guy Tracker
(p. 232)

microphone

alarm buzzer

battery
(other side)

sound recorder

speaker

NICK AND TESLA'S
SUPER-CYBORG GADGET GLOVE

"Has anyone seen Tesla's head?" Hiroko asked.

Nick Holt turned and stared at her in surprise.

"It's not here?" he asked Hiroko. "Uncle Newt had it just a minute ago."

Nick's uncle Newt was hunched over Tesla's hands, which lay palms up on the portable work bench in front of him.

"I did?" he said.

"Yeah. You had it tucked under your arm when you went to get a soda." It was Tesla Holt, Nick's twin sister, who answered this time. She said the words with her mouth, which was on her face, which was on her head. Which was attached to her neck.

Her arms still had hands on them, too.

Which meant it was the *other* Tesla in the room who was missing hands and a head. The animatronic Tesla, made to look like famous inventor Nikola Tesla. Of course, lacking his head and hands, he didn't look much like Nikola Tesla at the moment.

"Uh-oh," said Nick, whose full name was Nikola Copernicus Holt.

He and his twin sister, Tesla, each shared part of Nikola Tesla's name thanks to a family tradition handed down to their father, Albert Einstein Holt, from his father, Thomas Edison Holt.

"Why *uh-oh?*" asked Uncle Newt, a.k.a. Newton Galileo Holt.

Nick and Tesla didn't answer their uncle's question. They were already bolting for the nearest exit. They had a pretty good idea where animatronic Nikola Tesla's head had ended up—and why it would be a *really* good idea to retrieve it as soon as possible.

"Do you realize," Nick gasped to his sister as the two of them dashed toward the far end of the Hall of

Science, "that we weren't even supposed to be here today?" They passed Marie Curie sitting behind the wheel of one of the field hospital X-ray trucks she created to help wounded soldiers during World War I. "Uncle Newt and Hiroko finished their work two days ago."

Which was true. Their uncle and his kinda-sorta girlfriend Hiroko Sakurai were both robotics experts, and they'd been hired to save the exhibition after delays and malfunctions resulted in the firing of the original designer. The day before yesterday it seemed as though the job was all wrapped up.

"Well," Tesla said to her brother, "who did you expect the museum director to call this morning when she found out that Nikola Tesla's head was loose?" The pair slowed a bit to loop around René Descartes, who was lying in bed looking up at the fly that would inspire him to create the Cartesian coordinate system. "Plus, Charles Darwin had fallen over and crushed that flock of blue-footed boobies." She meant *models* of blue-footed boobies . . . blue-footed boobies being a species of seabird native to the South Pacific. "I mean, tonight's the museum's grand reopening!" Nick and Tesla skidded into a right turn past Percy Spencer, who was staring in wonderment at a glob of gooey chocolate, the first in the world to be melted by microwaves.

These were animatronic versions of famous scientists—manikins, basically, that were silent and motionless at the moment. But this very night they would move and speak thanks to computer-controlled mechanisms built inside them. Because tonight was the grand reopening of the Northern California Museum of Science, Industry, and Technology, which had been christened with a brand-new name: *The X-Treme Learnasium*. And the museum's centerpiece would be the Hall of Genius, where visitors could see and hear lifelike animatronic recreations of history's greatest thinkers.

Assuming the machines actually worked.

"I was hoping we'd be able to help," Nick answered glumly. Up ahead was Albert Einstein, posed in front of a chalkboard and writing his famous equation $E = mc^2$. Nick and Tesla both loved science and building things, but the animatronics were far too complex for them to work on. "All we've been able to do so far," Nick continued as they rounded the Einstein display, "is sweep up booby feathers."

The unmarked rear exit of the Hall of Science was hidden behind Einstein's chalkboard. The duo pushed open the door and burst through. "We are helping," Tesla told Nick. "We're going to rescue somebody from a heart attack."

On the other side of the doorway Nick and Tesla found themselves in the bright, white-walled, mazelike corridors that connected the exhibit galleries with the museum's offices, workshops, and storage rooms.

Tesla turned left, sprinted a few steps, and then suddenly spun on her heel and headed in the opposite direction.

"This way!" she said.

"Umm . . . ," Nick replied as he followed her.

A scream echoed down the hall from somewhere behind them.

"You were right the first time," Nick said.

Tesla whirled around again.

"Okay, then," she said. "*This way!*"

A few seconds later, after a right turn, a left turn, and a quick turnaround at a dead end, Nick and Tesla finally made it to their destination: the museum's small and cramped staff lunch room. There was just one table, and one counter, and one microwave, and one refrigerator.

And one woman, who was standing in front of the open fridge and staring down at something nestled between a six-pack of soda cans and some Tupperware.

The woman turned. "Nikola Tesla's head," she growled. "In the fridge, next to my tarragon chicken salad."

"Wow, impressive! You recognized him!" Nick said, smiling feebly.

He didn't get a smile in return, feeble or otherwise. Which didn't come as a surprise.

The woman was Ellen Wharton-Wheeler, the museum's chief curator. When Nick and Tesla met her briefly earlier that morning, her only response to Uncle Newt's introduction had been a clipped "This isn't an amusement park, no matter what certain people seem to think."

"She's not a fan of the Hall of Genius," Hiroko had whispered as the woman stomped off.

"She doesn't seem like a fan of *people*," Nick had whispered back.

Now Ellen Wharton-Wheeler was frowning at

Nick and Tesla as though they didn't even qualify as people. She seemed to consider them more like cockroaches—nasty little intruders sullying her pristine and perfect world.

"Is this some kind of practical joke?" she snapped at the kids. She was a tall, husky, imposing woman. And now she was holding the phony head of Nikola Tesla as if she was about to pelt Nick and Tesla with it, dodgeball-style.

"Oh, no!" Nick replied. "It was just an accident!"

"Our uncle had it with him when he came to get a soda out of the refrigerator," Tesla added. "And . . . well . . . he's *really* forgetful. Last week he—" Tesla was about to describe the time Uncle Newt absent-mindedly swapped a container of ice cream for a beaker of sulfuric acid, resulting in a freezer full of half-dissolved cardboard and liquefied Hot Pockets. But before she could, two boys came charging into the room. One was short and slim, the other tall and beefy.

"Has it started? Has it started?" asked the bigger one. It was Nick and Tesla's friend Silas.

The smaller of the two boys—their friend De-Marco—pointed at the head in Wharton-Wheeler's

hands.

"Whoa! You were right, Silas! They already had to kill one!"

"I told you it was just a matter of time," Silas replied. Then he peered anxiously over his shoulder. "Are there more?"

"What is he talking about?" Wharton-Wheeler asked. She directed the question at Nick and Tesla, as if they'd suddenly been upgraded. Maybe they were cockroaches, but at least they weren't crazy.

"I'm sorry, ma'am. This is all just a big misunderstanding," Nick said because he *really* didn't want to explain what Silas and DeMarco were talking about.

All day, Silas had been insisting that the animatronic figures in the Hall of Genius were robots. Which meant that sooner or later, he believed, they'd do what robots inevitably do: rise up, destroy their human masters, and take over the world.

Silas read *a lot* of comic books. In fact, his father owned a comic-book store.

"If you'll just give us the head," Tesla said, "we'll get out of your hair."

Wharton-Wheeler squinted as if trying to decide whether they were pulling a prank. But after ten seconds or so, she seemed to decide she didn't care.

She tossed Nikola Tesla's head across the room.

"Oooh, yikes! Fragile!" Nick squeaked.

Fortunately, she was throwing the head into the outstretched arms of Tesla Holt, where it landed safe and sound.

"Go on," Wharton-Wheeler said, "take that back to your uncle. At least Nikola Tesla will have a good head on his shoulders, even if no one else around here does."

"What do you have against our uncle?" Tesla

asked her.

It was then that the curator's cold expression warmed, if just the teeniest bit. She still looked frosty, though.

"I don't have anything against your uncle," she said. "I wouldn't even have anything against what he's doing . . . if he were doing it at a county fair. That's a funhouse he's working on. What used to be a serious, respectable museum is being turned into a tacky tourist trap, and I for one am not going to stand silently by while a once-great institution is—"

As she spoke the volume of her voice had been rising, rising, rising, but she cut herself off just before reaching shriek levels. Then she took a deep breath and patted down her short graying hair, even though it wasn't mussed.

"Oh, well," she continued, calmly. "At least my new exhibit is ready on time. Which means I don't have to sit here eating chicken salad if I don't want to. And suddenly, I don't want to. I'm going out for lunch."

She closed the refrigerator and started strutting so briskly toward the door that Silas and DeMarco had to jump out of the way or risk being bowled over.

"Wow, lady," DeMarco said once she was gone. "Tell us what you *really* think."

Silas shook his head. "How could anyone hate robots that much? They're probably gonna destroy the human race and all, but they're still cool."

"Where have you two been?" Nick asked his friends. "You went to the bathroom half an hour ago."

DeMarco and Silas answered at the same time:

"We got lost we were exploring!"

Nick assumed they were both telling the truth—they probably got lost and then used that as an excuse to poke around. Silas and DeMarco weren't as interested in science and gadgetry as Nick and Tesla were. They were more interested in finding innovative new uses for firecrackers and restaging ill-advised stunts they'd seen on YouTube. The two of them had only tagged along to the museum because DeMarco's little sisters were making him miserable and Silas wanted a front-row seat for the beginning of what he called "Robo-geddon." After a couple hours in the Hall of Genius with no robot rebellion to battle, the two boys had grown very, very bored.

"Well, don't go wandering off again," Nick lectured them. "Uncle Newt may have gotten permission for us to hang with him today, but certain people probably wouldn't mind having us thrown out."

"Oh? Like who?" asked Silas.

Nick jerked a thumb at the door. "Uh, like maybe the woman who was just ranting about Uncle Newt's 'funhouse'?"

"Oh, yeah," said Silas. "Her."

"Come on," Tesla said, starting toward the hall. "We've gotta get this head back to the Hall of Genius."

She stepped out into the corridor and took a quick left.

"This way," she said.

"Umm . . . ," said Nick.

After a few more steps, Tesla turned around.

"Right," she said. "*This way.*"

They continued for a bit and then Tesla led the boys around a corner, nearly walking right into another person.

"Whoa!" she blurted out, stopping suddenly in her tracks. She was hugging the Tesla head tightly so that it wouldn't drop. Her sudden stop caused Nick to nearly collide with her, which in turn caused

DeMarco to nearly collide with Nick. Silas had been trailing farther behind, half-expecting they'd all have to change direction again, so he was in no danger of colliding with anyone.

When all the kids had regained their footing, they found themselves facing a squat, dark-haired, broad-chested man wearing a loose-fitting purple muscle shirt and acid-washed jeans. His arms and chest bulged with veiny muscles, which were so huge he looked like an overinflated balloon animal. The museum, or at least the exhibition space, was mostly deserted while final preparations were being made for the reopening, so the kids had seen only a few people on the premises. None of them had looked anything like this guy.

The stranger gaped in disbelief at the head in Tesla's hands, but only for a second. His confused expression quickly changed to one of glee.

"All right, punks," he snarled through a barely suppressed smirk. "Drop the head, and nobody gets hurt!"

2

"Excuse me?" asked Tesla, stunned.

It wasn't every day she was called a punk. In fact, until now there had never been *any* day when she'd been called a punk.

The muscle-bound man wasn't tall, but with his overpumped arms akimbo and legs spread wide in some kind of martial arts stance, he seemed to fill the entire hallway.

"I said: all right, punks," he repeated slowly. "Drop the head and . . ."

The man's smirk faded and his words trailed off.

"Nobody gets hurt," Silas finished

for him helpfully.

"Yeah. Right," the man said, sounding distract-ed. He was squinting at the pink laminated badges hanging around the boys' necks. (Tesla was wear-ing one, too, but it was hidden by the head she was holding.)

The badges said VISITOR.

"So," the man continued, "you managed to steal yourself some day passes, huh?" His voice had lost all its energy; he was speaking in a half-hearted sort of way, as if he didn't believe his own accusation. "Very clever for a bunch of kids," he added. "But not clever enough to fool Berg." He tapped his chest with his thumb. "Me, that is."

"We didn't steal the badges, Mr. Berg!" Nick pro-tested. "Our uncle got them for us! Newton Holt. He's working in the Hall of Genius with Hiroko Sakurai right now."

"Are you talking about . . . the scientist lady and the dude with the doctor's coat and the bad hair?" Berg asked, his eyes narrowing.

Nick noted Berg's greasy slicked-back locks, which ended in a stubby ponytail sprouting from the back of his neck. Uncle Newt's wild mane did tend to defy gravity, but this guy wasn't in any position to criticize other people's hairstyles. Nick decided to keep his opinion to himself.

"Yes," Nick said. "That's them."

The man sighed.

"All right, then. I guess you're okay," he said. "Sorry about the 'punks' thing. I thought you were scumball vandals who'd snuck in to trash the place."

"Have you had trouble with scumball vandals?" asked DeMarco. He actually seemed excited by the idea that hooligan gangs might be roaming the museum.

"No," Berg said, sounding extremely disappointed. "But there was a rumor going around, a week or so back, about people maybe prowling around."

"What was the rumor?" Tesla asked.

The man shrugged. "That there were people maybe prowling around. That was all I heard, anyway. They don't tell me much 'cuz I'm the low man on the totem pole around here. That's why I'm stuck patrolling all the boring stuff while everyone else is guarding the you-know-what."

"The you-know-what?" said Nick.

"You know." Berg winked at him. "The you-know-what."

"We don't know what the you-know-what is," said Nick.

"We didn't even know there was a you-know-what," said Tesla.

"I don't know what any of you are talking about," said Silas.

DeMarco just shrugged.

Berg blinked at the kids for a moment. "You don't know about the you-know-what?" he asked them.

They all shook their heads.

"Oh," Berg said. He was quiet for a few seconds. "In that case, forget I mentioned it."

"So are you a security guard or something?" Nick asked. Considering Berg's sleeveless shirt and acid-washed jeans, Nick thought he looked more like a bouncer at a heavy-metal concert than a rent-a-cop. But again, he decided to keep his opinion to himself.

"Yes," Berg answered, straightening a bit. "I'm a private patrol officer for the Learnasium. A new one . . . and a late one. I can never find the changing room around here. Anyway, bye!"

With that, he scooted around Tesla and the others and lumbered off down the hallway.

"I think he's going the wrong way," said Silas.

"Oh, well," said DeMarco. "Maybe he'll finally find those scumball vandals he's hoping for."

"Come on." Tesla started walking up the hall again. "Hiroko and Uncle Newt are still waiting for this head."

Nick noticed that his sister wasn't walking as quickly as before. And that her eyes had a certain distant, distracted look.

Nick knew what that meant. And it made him nervous. Because he was positive that his sister was thinking this:

So there's a you-know-what around here, huh? Maybe we should find out exactly what this you-know-what is. . . .

"For the thousandth time, Silas," Nick said. "Animatronic figures are *not* robots."

The kids had found their way back to the Hall of Genius, where they were watching Uncle Newt and Hiroko reheading the beheaded Nikola Tesla.

"Robots can do stuff," Nick went on. "Build things or explore places or dispose of bombs or whatever." Silas looked unconvinced, so Nick added, "Like those robot insects we built that one time."

"They really did stuff," DeMarco chimed in. "They freaked out that guy who was afraid of bugs."

Nick ignored DeMarco and waved his hand at a nearby display, which showed the Renaissance physiologist Sanctorius Sanctorius seated in the hanging chair that he used to measure his weight every day for thirty years. (It's not that Sanctorius was on a strict diet; he was trying to understand human metabolism.) When the Hall of Genius animatronics were activated, the weighing chair would move slowly up and down while Sanctorius gnawed on a rubber chicken leg. "These animatronics are cool," Nick said, "but basically they're just fancy decorations."

"*Robotic* decorations," Silas insisted, "that look like people! I'm telling you, this is just asking for a robot uprising. Haven't you ever seen a *Terminator* movie?"

"Hey," DeMarco interrupted, "when robots look like people, doesn't that make them cyborgs?"

Nick shook his head. "Cyborgs are people with machine parts that enhance their abilities. Robots that look human are called androids."

"That's it," DeMarco said. "Mandroids."

"*Androids,*" Nick corrected.

"They always turn evil, too," Silas said.

Nick sighed. He was glad Tesla had bailed on this conversation and drifted away to give Nikola Tesla's hands one last look before they were reattached to his body. Nick had no fear of robots running amok, but if his sister had to listen to Silas babbling about it much longer, *she* might go berserk.

There was no danger of Tesla hearing Silas at the moment. She loved robotics more than anything, except for her mom and dad, and maybe lemon macadamia nut cookies, and she'd been fascinated by the mechanical hands since she first laid eyes on them. Nick glanced her way as Silas described the telltale signs that a robot was about to turn evil, and he saw that his sister still had the same pensive, faraway look he'd noticed in the hallway.

Tesla, Nick realized, was still stewing over their conversation with Berg, the muscle-headed guard.

If there's one thing you should never say to

Tesla Holt, it's "I know something you don't know." Because before long, she'll find a way to make that statement untrue.

Case in point: the plaque that accompanied the Nikola Tesla display. About a quarter of the text had been covered with duct tape, as if someone was trying to censor part of the scientist's life. When Tesla had noticed, she asked Uncle Newt and Hiroko about it, but they didn't have a clue. They were just there to fix the animatronics. Ever since, Tesla had a tendency to drift over to the display, where she'd pick idly at the edges of the duct tape on the sign until Nick told her to stop.

And now Tesla had something new to pick at:

What was the you-know-what?

"Hey, Tez," Uncle Newt called to her. "Hand me those hands, would you?"

"Huh, what? Hands?" said Tesla, snapping back to the here and now. "Oh, sure."

She picked up the animatronic hands from the worktable and walked them across the room. Uncle Newt took one hand, Hiroko took the other, and they inserted them into the white cuffs poking from the sleeves of the figure's frock coat. There was a *click* and a *clack,* and then Uncle Newt and Hiroko stepped back and grinned at each other.

"Success!" said Uncle Newt.

"Well, maybe," said Hiroko. "We should probably make sure he still works."

"Hmm. Good idea."

Uncle Newt walked to a nearby table covered with petri dishes and test tubes and opened a drawer. Inside were a computer screen and a keyboard and a phone—the hidden control station for the Hall of Genius.

Uncle Newt started typing on the keyboard. As he worked, Sir Alexander Fleming, discoverer of penicillin, stared at him with unblinking eyes from the other side of the table. Like Uncle Newt, Fleming wore a white lab coat, though beneath his was a dark suit, compared to Uncle Newt's typical outfit of jeans and a moth-eaten, ketchup-stained T-shirt.

"Here comes the power," Uncle Newt said.

There was a low humming sound. Then, one by one, spotlights came on all around the Hall of Genius.

Despite the name, the exhibition space wasn't a hallway at all. It was a large teardrop-shaped room with an entrance/exit at the narrow end. Animatronic figures and their information plaques lined the curving walls, and in the center was the biggest display—the Wright brothers set to launch their first airplane and, looming above them, a flying machine designed and piloted by Leonardo da Vinci.

"Annnnnnd . . . go!" said Uncle Newt. He punched Enter on the keyboard.

For two seconds, everyone was absolutely quiet, even Silas. Then the propellers on the Wright brothers' plane started to turn. Johannes Gutenberg's printing press began stamping out pages of the forty-two-line Bible. The cylinder on Thomas Edison's phonograph started spinning, and the inventor's own voice could be heard saying, "Mary had a little lamb whose fleece was white as snow." All around the room, animatronic scientists and philosophers and inventors began picking up test tubes, leaning over microscopes, tinkering with machinery, and even—in the case of a towel-wrapped Archimedes, the person who discovered liquid displacement—dipping a foot into a bathtub and opening his eyes wide as the cellophane "water" rose up over his ankle.

"Whoa!" said Nick.

"Wow!" said Tesla.

"Cool!" said DeMarco.

"Creepy," muttered Silas.

Hiroko walked over to Uncle Newt and, smiling, gave him a high five.

"Now we just need to make sure Nikola Tesla has his head screwed on right, then we can go home," said Uncle Newt. He turned to his niece. "Tez, would you do the honors?"

Tesla grinned. "I'd love to."

She and Nick had been hearing about the animatronic figures all week, ever since the X-Treme Learnasium first called Uncle Newt to see if he could come in for an emergency last-minute overhaul of the Hall of Genius. But now would be her first chance to really see one of the figures in action. (Instead of bringing along Tesla and Nick to be his helpers, like they'd wanted, Uncle Newt had foisted the two of them onto Silas's family and recruited Hiroko to assist at the museum—just because she used to be a robotics specialist at NASA, like Uncle Newt. Nick and Tesla pouted for days afterward.)

Tesla walked over to the information display in

front of her namesake. Printed on the sign was the scientist's (partially tape-covered) biography, along with an explanation of the scene the animatronic figure was enacting: Tesla demonstrating one of his inventions at the 1893 World's Columbian Exposition in Chicago.

Beside the text was a big red button.

Tesla reached out and pushed it.

"Hello," the mechanical Tesla said in a heavily accented voice. "Would you like me to show you how an induction motor works?"

"Yes," answered Tesla.

"Excellent," said the animatronic Tesla. "It is really quite interesting."

Tesla gave Uncle Newt and Hiroko a thumbs-up. The voice-recognition software was working perfectly.

"The key," Nikola Tesla went on, "is creating a rotating magnetic field."

"You were right, Silas. The robots are dangerous," DeMarco grumbled. "That one's about to bore me to death."

Nick shushed him.

"Hello!" boomed a voice behind the three boys.

"Eee!" said Nick.

"Aaa!" said DeMarco.

"Whoa, whoa, whoa!" said Silas.

The three of them whipped around to see a man in an old-fashioned suit and clunky headphones staring at them as he fiddled with a black box studded with gauges and dials.

"Would you like-a to hear-a how I create-a the wireless?" the man said in a ridiculously thick Italian accent. "It all began-a with the discovery of a-radio waves-a."

"Who is *that*?" DeMarco asked as the animatronic man droned on.

"It's Marconi," said Nick. "The guy who invented radio."

"He sounds more like one of the Super Mario brothers," said Silas.

"Is the accent too much?" Uncle Newt called out from the other side of the Hall of Genius.

Hiroko put a hand on his arm.

"I wouldn't worry about the accent, Newt," she said. "Why is Marconi talking at all?"

"Well, obviously the kids activated him. Right, boys?"

Nick, Silas, and DeMarco all shook their heads.

"We didn't touch a thing," said Nick.

"Oh," said Uncle Newt.

Uh-oh, said the look on his face.

"Hello!" said another voice. This one came from a portly, balding man wearing little round granny glasses. "Would you like to hear the truth about my experiments with electricity and lightning?"

It was Benjamin Franklin, holding a kite and a key. He immediately launched into a lecture about lightning and electricity. Meanwhile, Nikola Tesla and Marconi kept talking.

"Uh . . . are the animatronics starting to turn on by themselves?" Tesla asked.

"They're not supposed to," Uncle Newt answered.

"Hello," said Eli Whitney, inventor of the cotton gin.

"Hello," said pioneering microbiologist Louis Pasteur.

"Hello," said anthropologists Louis and Mary Leakey.

"Hello," said primatologists Dian Fossey and Jane Goodall.

"Hello," said Johannes Kepler and Carl Sagan and

Stephen Hawking and Isaac Asimov . . .

In a few more seconds, every animatronic figure in the Hall of Genius was talking and moving, all of them explaining and demonstrating their discoveries.

Uncle Newt began typing frantically on the keyboard.

"I don't understand," he said. "According to the control dashboard, none of this is happening."

"Well, it is!" Hiroko said.

She had to shout to be heard over the din of scientific explanations.

Then the animatronic figures began talking louder. And faster.

"People remember me mostlyforthecottongin," Eli Whitney spat out, the pitch of his voice rising to a squeak as his words sped up. "ButIalsohelpedrevolutionizemanufacturingbypopularizingtheuseofinterchangeableparts!"

"Ugh!" DeMarco moaned, slapping his hands over his ears. "It's like being screamed at by fifty Mickey Mouses!"

The animatronics were moving so fast that several of them began to wobble.

"Turn them off! Turn them off!" yelled Hiroko.

"I can't! I can't!" Uncle Newt yelled back, still typing furiously.

A beaker flew out of Louis Pasteur's hand, shooting past Nick's head.

Charles Darwin's head fell off and crushed another blue-footed booby.

"Arobotmaynotinjureahumanbeingorthroughinactionallowahumanbeingtocometoharm," Isaac Asimov screeched, and then he toppled over. Right onto Nick and DeMarco.

"It's here!" Silas screamed. "Robo-geddon!"

And then the whole room went black.

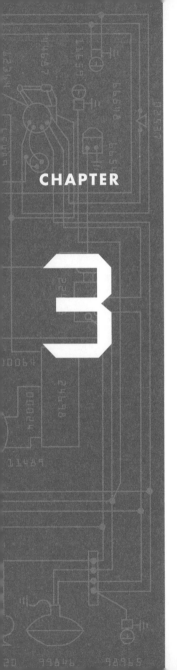

When the lights went out, the shrill jabbering of the animatronics came to a sudden stop. For a few moments, the only sound in the utter darkness of the Hall of Genius was a low groaning.

Then slow, stumbling steps.

Then a heavy thump.

"If that's a robot," Silas said, "I surrender."

"It's not a robot," said Tesla. "It's me getting Nick and DeMarco out from under Isaac Asimov."

"Thanks for the help, Silas," DeMarco added sarcastically.

"Sorry, man," Silas mumbled.

"Nick, are you okay?" Uncle Newt asked. "I'd come help Tesla, but I'm afraid I'd step on you."

"It's okay, I'm fine," Nick said. "But wow—those robots are heavier than they look."

"Ha," Silas said half-heartedly. "You called it a robot."

"Oh, shut up," Nick shot back.

There was more movement in the dark, and then something bumped into Uncle Newt and Hiroko from behind.

"Yah!" said Uncle Newt.

"Sorry. It's just me again," said Tesla. "I wanted to see if the controls were still on."

"No. There's no power to anything," Hiroko said. "We won't know what happened until—oooh, my eyes!"

Just as abruptly as they'd gone out, the lights turned back on.

Everyone spent the next few seconds blinking and rubbing their eyes. Then, one by one, they turned to stare uneasily at the animatronic figures surrounding them.

The animatronics were motionless. Dead.

"Well," Nick said, "if that was Robo-geddon, I

guess it's over."

Silas walked over to the toppled Isaac Asimov figure and prodded it with his toe. He looked almost disappointed when the scientist and science-fiction writer didn't push himself up and lunge at him.

"I don't know," Silas said. "There's always that moment when you think the evil robot has finally been defeated, but then its eyes start glowing red and *whammo!*"

He gave the figure on the floor another poke, but there was no whammo.

The sound of quick footsteps rose from somewhere in the distance, and soon a man and a woman came hustling into the Hall of Genius. They were about the same age, maybe a decade younger than the forty-ish Uncle Newt and Hiroko. The man was dressed in a T-shirt, an unbuttoned and untucked lumberjack shirt, and wrinkled jeans. His hair was short and messy, and even his thick glasses sat slightly askew on his confused face. The woman had the opposite appearance: she wore a tidy businessy-type suit, her hair was carefully styled, and her face bore the confident expression of someone who was in charge—and knew it.

"Oh, hello," said Uncle Newt as calmly as if two neighbors had just stopped by to chat. In reality, none of Uncle Newt's real neighbors ever stopped by to chat, mostly because of the explosive noises, strange clouds of smoke, and other phenomena that tended to erupt from his basement laboratory. "Kids," he continued, "meet Katherine Mavis, the Learnasium's executive director, and—"

"What are you guys doing here?" the man interrupted. "I thought the Hall of Genius was finished."

"I tasked them to come in today for some last-minute R&R of the exhibition, Mr. Jones," the director explained to her slovenly dressed companion. His confused look became even more confused, so she added, "Rehab and repair." Then Mavis looked down at Charles Darwin's head, which was lying on the floor near her feet. The head stared back, booby feathers tangled in its hair. She turned around slowly, regarding all the other heads, hands, and props littering the hall, shaken loose when the animatronics went wild. "What happened here? It sounded like a riot broke out!"

"A riot of chipmunks," Jones added.

"I'm sorry," Hiroko said, looking profoundly

embarrassed. "We don't know what went wrong. We powered everything up so we could test one of the animatronics, and then the whole exhibit started going nuts."

Jones squinted at Hiroko through the thick lenses of his fashionably clunky black-framed glasses. He looked like he hadn't shaved in days, and his dark gel-slathered hair stood straight up on end, as if he just stuck his finger in an electrical outlet.

The words MIGRAINE MONKEY MISSLE TEST were printed across the front of his T-shirt, beneath a drawing of a depressed-looking chimp riding a saddled rocket.

"The exhibit started going nuts?" Jones echoed. "I'm sorry, but what exactly does that mean in technical terms?"

"The pneumatics, hydraulics, and sound files all activated simultaneously and then accelerated so far beyond their performance parameters that some of the animatronics probably burned out their motion actuators," Hiroko said.

"You know. Going nuts!" Uncle Newt added. "My theory is that . . . uhh . . ."

His face went blank, and he rubbed his chin for

a moment. Then he said, "Whaddaya know. I don't even have a theory."

Jones sighed, scratching the first "M" on his Migraine Monkey Missile Test shirt. "Well," he said, "let's see what I can come up with."

He walked over to the control screen—which had reactivated when the lights turned back on—and began typing, hard and fast.

"Fine. Fine. Fine. Fine. *Fine*," he said as he typed and a flurry of login screens and control panels and dashboards and graphs came and went with eye-blistering speed. "I don't see anything wrong with the network access control, and there's nothing on the servers that would explain why an exhibit would 'go nuts.'"

Then he glanced over his shoulder and eyed Tesla with suspicion.

"You didn't let someone play around with the controls, did you?" he said to Uncle Newt.

"No!" Uncle Newt replied indignantly.

He thought it over a moment before adding, "I was saving that for later."

Jones gave Uncle Newt an "Are you kidding me?" look.

"Hey, they're smart kids!" Uncle Newt said. "Well, most of them."

Silas and DeMarco glowered at him. "Not cool, man," Silas grumbled.

"If you don't mind my asking," Jones said, "why do you have kids in here at all?"

"Dr. Holt's niece and nephew are habitating with him this summer," Mavis answered. "He didn't have anyone queued up to macromanage them today because he thought the project was end-cycled. So I greenlit his request for permission to bring them in, along with a couple friends."

"Oh. Okay then," Jones answered. But he didn't seem to mean it.

"This is my niece and nephew, by the way—Tesla and Nick," Uncle Newt said. "And their friends Sirius and Dijon."

"Silas and DeMarco," Hiroko corrected.

"Kids," Uncle Newt continued obliviously, "meet Mojo Jones, the—"

"Let me guess," Nick cut in. "Chief technology officer?"

"No," said Jones, sounding annoyed.

"Database administrator?" Tesla said.

"No," he said again, sounding even more annoyed.

"Network engineer?" said Nick.

"No," he said, sounding quite fed up with the questions. "I'm the—"

"Senior system manager?" Tesla quickly interrupted.

"No! I mean yes!" said Jones, his annoyance replaced by surprised. "How'd you know?"

Tesla shrugged. "There are only so many names for the computer guy, and it's obvious that's what you are." She threw a gloating glance at her brother. "Beat ya to it!"

"Senior system administrator was my next guess," Nick said.

Jones and Mavis looked at each other. Obviously, Newt's description of the kids was no exaggeration: they *were* smart.

"Well, it's nice to meet you," Jones said, sounding almost friendly this time. "But I wish it were under better circumstances. Whatever just happened in here blew out the power for the whole museum and messed up all kinds of very important systems. I thought I was ready for the reopening, but now . . ."

He shook his head hopelessly, looking almost as despondent as the Migraine Monkey on his T-shirt.

"Do you think you can ideate the problem and get it one-eightied in time for the rededication gala tonight?" Mavis asked Uncle Newt and Hiroko.

"Absolutely!" Uncle Newt said.

"Assuming we can figure out what went wrong in the first place," Hiroko added, with about a quarter of the confidence.

Their answers didn't leave the director looking very reassured. "Tonight's the rollout of our new branding," she said. "Our chance to reposition ourselves in an extremely mediagenic way in what's become an aggressively competitive environment for the infotainment side of the urban facility-based destination market. We can't afford any negative messaging just as we're establishing a whole new public profile."

"Was that English?" Silas said quietly to DeMarco. But not quietly enough.

"Tonight's a big night for the Learnasium," Jones translated for him. "It would be really bad—for *everyone involved*—if things 'went nuts' again."

"Understood! No worries! It's as good as fixed!"

Uncle Newt said enthusiastically.

Hiroko managed a feeble smile but looked like she wanted to throw up.

"Well then," the director said, "we'll leave you to it. Come on, Mojo," she added. "We'd better go check on the *mmm mmm mmmmm*."

She said the last three words with her lips sealed.

"Right," said Jones, and they turned to go. As they hustled out of the hall, the director called back: "Keep me in the loop on your progress, Dr. Holt. If I need to proactively downgrade stakeholder expectations for the paradigm shift we can expect to leverage from tonight's infovent, I'll want plenty of runway time."

"Aye, aye!" Uncle Newt replied with a crisp salute. "Whatever that meant, I'm on it."

Mavis did not salute back.

"Great," Jones could be heard murmuring to her as they left the Hall of Genius. "It's Mark Carstairs all over again."

Nick and Tesla looked at each other. They waited patiently till the director and Mojo Jones were out of earshot, then they simultaneously turned toward their uncle to ask the question each knew the other was thinking.

"Who's Mark Carstairs?"

"An old colleague of mine," Uncle Newt said, sighing. "Smart guy. Heck of a saxophone player, too. He used to take requests at Christmas parties. The only time I ever saw him stumped was when someone asked for—"

"More important," Hiroko broke in, "Mark was the original designer of the Hall of Genius. He oversaw the building of the animatronics and all the construction. But then there were problems, and he was fired."

"Like *these* kinds of problems?" Tesla asked, waving a hand at Isaac Asimov, who was still lying facedown on the floor.

"Sort of," Hiroko said. "There was trouble with the control mechanisms. Nothing this extreme, though." She turned to Uncle Newt. "Do you really think we can figure out what's wrong and have everything ready again by tonight?"

"Not really!" Uncle Newt said with a smile. "But don't you just love my can-do attitude?"

"What did that Jones guy mean about it being bad for everyone if the Hall of Genius doesn't work?"

Nick asked.

"The museum just spent millions on new exhibits," Hiroko explained. "If something goes wrong at the rededication, it'll be a huge black eye for them." She turned a worried look on Uncle Newt. "And for us. With a project this big and expensive, there's bound to be news coverage if it all falls apart. We'll be laughingstocks."

Uncle Newt swiped a hand at her dismissively.

"Laughingstocks shmaffing-bocks! I don't care about that!" He walked over to animatronic Albert Einstein and picked up the chalk that had fallen from the figure's hand. "I just don't want to let these guys down."

He gave it a hearty slap on the back.

Einstein's left arm fell off.

"Oops," said Uncle Newt. "Sorry, Al."

Hiroko walked over to Uncle Newt as he bent down to retrieve the loose arm.

"Is there any way we can help?" Nick asked.

"No," Hiroko said with a sigh. "I'm afraid not."

"I think there is," Tesla said, her voice too low for the adults to hear. Besides which, they were too busy reattaching Einstein's arm to notice.

Tesla motioned for Nick, Silas, and DeMarco to join her by one of the displays on the other side of the hall—the office of Sigmund Freud, the pioneer of modern psychiatry, to be specific.

"I think it's up to us to make sure the Hall of Genius doesn't break down again," Tesla said as the others gathered around.

"Us?" said Silas.

"What can we do?" said DeMarco. "We don't know anything about fixing robots."

"Animatronics," Nick corrected for the twentieth time that day.

"We don't know anything about that either," said Silas.

Tesla crossed her arms and frowned at the boys.

"Don't you get it? It's not animatronics or robotics that's the problem," she said. "It's sabotage!"

"What?" said DeMarco.

"Huh?" said Silas.

"Of course," said Nick.

Tesla turned a grim smile on her brother.

"What else could it be but sabotage, am I right?" she said to Nick. Then she noticed he was rolling his eyes. "What's that look for?"

"I wasn't saying, 'Sabotage! Of course!'" Nick explained. "I was saying, 'Tesla *thinks* it's sabotage. Of course.'"

"And what's that supposed to mean?"

"Look . . . just sit down for a

second, would you?"

Nick pointed to the couch in Freud's office. The gray-bearded father of psychoanalysis sat in a chair nearby, watching thoughtfully, a fake cigar in the fingers of one fake hand.

Tesla scowled.

"We don't have time for—"

"Sit," Nick broke in firmly. Firm wasn't his usual style, so Tesla did as her brother asked. But she didn't drop the scowl.

"Tez," Nick said, "ever since we came to live with Uncle Newt, you've been looking for trouble—"

"And finding it," DeMarco said. Tesla turned her scowl DeMarco's way, prompting him to close his mouth very tight.

"What have we done so far with our summer vacation?" Nick asked. "Catch kidnappers! Fight spies! Battle rampaging robots!"

"See! Told ya robots were evil!" Silas said.

Now it was Nick's turn to scowl. Silas shrugged but said nothing more.

"And do you know *why* we keep getting into one mess after another?" Nick continued.

"A combination of bad luck and the fact that

our parents are on the run because they seem to be working on some sort of super-secret government project that foreign agents are trying to get their hands on even though we thought they were experts on watering soybeans?" Tesla said.

"Good recap," said DeMarco.

Nick was shaking his head.

"It's because you're so worried about Mom and Dad, and so frustrated that we can't do anything about whatever's happened to them, that you keep looking for problems you think you *can* solve."

"That's ridiculous," Tesla said with a snort.

Nick raised his eyebrows and stroked his chin.

"Is it?"

"*Yes!*"

Tesla didn't mean to shout it, but she did.

Uncle Newt didn't seem to notice the yelling, which wasn't unusual. More than once he hadn't detected when his own lab coat was on fire. But Hiroko looked up from the hand she was trying to reattach to George Washington Carver.

The kids smiled and waved.

Hiroko returned the wave glumly and returned to work.

"Look, Nick," Tesla said, fighting to keep her voice low, "just because we're twins doesn't mean you can read my mind. This isn't some dumb obsession. It's logic. The grown-ups are just too busy to stop and think it through."

"What's so logical about it?" Nick said. "Some super-complicated machinery keeps breaking down. Why does that have to be sabotage?"

"Because it wasn't a mechanical failure, was it? The animatronics were working fine. They just started going way too fast. The displays are all controlled by computer, and all the computers in the museum are part of a network. Well, how hard could it be for someone to get access to the controls and crank 'em up too high?"

"Pretty darn hard, actually, if that Mojo Jones guy is doing his job right."

"But what if we're talking about someone who already had access to the network? Someone with a grudge against the Hall of Genius or the X-Treme Learnasium?"

Nick started to say something, then stopped himself instead and pondered for a moment.

"Like Carstairs, the fired designer," he said. "You

think he might be out for revenge?"

"Or what's-her-name. Mrs. Wheeler-Dealer!" De-Marco added.

"Wharton-Wheeler," Tesla corrected.

"Right," said DeMarco. "The grouchy curator lady. She hates the Hall of Genius."

"Or that bodybuilder security guard guy," Silas said. "Obviously, he thirsts for vengeance because, uh, he's bitter about, um . . ."

"Getting lost in the halls all the time and not being allowed to guard the you-know-what," DeMarco suggested.

"Forget the security guard," Tesla said. "We've got two strong suspects, and that's enough. Don't you think?"

She stared hard at her brother.

"I don't know," he said. "Maybe."

Tesla hopped up, took her brother by the shoulders, and *forced him* to sit on the couch.

"Tell me, Nick," she said. "Why won't you accept the obvious—that there's a saboteur in the museum?"

"Because it's not obvious," Nick said. "And I'm tired of all the trouble we keep getting into. It makes me think our lives are never gonna get back to normal."

Nick stretched out flat on the couch and clasped his hands on his chest.

"I just want things to be like they used to. I wish we were back home in Virginia with Mom and Dad and—"

Tesla grabbed his hands and yanked him off the couch.

"All right, all right. We can get into all that later," she said. "Right now we have to save Uncle Newt and Hiroko's professional reputations!"

"I do want to help Uncle Newt and Hiroko," Nick admitted. "Sounds like this could be real trouble for them."

"Exactly," Tesla said. "We have to catch the bad guy and rescue the museum."

"Yippee. Another adventure," Nick said with a groan. "I don't know why people think adventures are so cool. In fact, they're really stressful."

"Stress is fun!" DeMarco enthused.

"Yeah!" said Silas.

"Well, I'm glad you guys think so," Nick said. "Because something tells me we're in for a lot more quote-unquote fun."

But DeMarco and Silas weren't listening anymore. They were following Tesla toward the exit.

Nick sighed. And then he followed, too.

Unlike the back door behind Albert Einstein's chalkboard, the official entrance to the Hall of Genius consisted of two tall white sliding doors that reached all the way to the high ceiling. For the gala that night, they'd be pushed into recesses in the walls, but at the moment they were nearly closed, with only a three-foot gap between them. Just enough space for the kids to pass through.

One by one, they stepped into the museum's cavernous atrium lobby. It was a dark and murky place. The ceiling was mostly glass panels, but little light was getting through on this overcast day. Plus, all the lights were turned off to save energy until it was time for the rededication soirée. The result was that the atrium had all the cheer of a tomb.

Visible through the gloom were the vague outlines of various displays and activity booths. The open space was dotted with a pendulum and a zoetrope here, a holographic sculpture and a camera obscura there, as well as gyroscopes and periscopes and kinetoscopes and pretty much every other scope known to humanity. Around the perimeter of the atrium loomed large lumpy shapes that seemed like rolling gray hills but were in fact giant foam-rubber reproductions of just about every organ in the human body.

At the center of it all stood a life-size re-creation of a Tyrannosaurus rex locked in a battle to the death with a bloodied triceratops. According to Uncle Newt, the dinosaurs were animatronic, too. During visiting hours, the Learnasium would pipe in their roars and shrieks, along with the sound of stomping feet and ripping flesh.

"'Cause, you know . . . X-Treme, right?" he'd added.

But for now the dinosaurs—and the exhibits surrounding them—were eerily quiet. All sides of the atrium featured entrances to the museum wings that held the larger exhibits, like the Hall of Genius. Most of the other wings were open but dark. The Hall of Genius was blocked by the big partition doors, as were two other exhibit spaces. One of the closed-off areas was on the other side of the dinosaurs, and the other was at the top of a flight of wide, open stairs that led to a second floor equipped with a balcony that jutted over the gift shop.

"Well," Nick said, "where do we start?"

"At the moment, there's not much we can do about Carstairs," Tesla said. "He's not here."

"As far as *we know*," DeMarco added, speaking in an overly ominous voice that most people reserve for telling ghost stories.

"But Ms. Wharton-Wheeler works right here in this building somewhere," Tesla plowed on. "We need to figure out where her office is so we can—"

"Hold it right there, punks!" barked a voice from the darkness. "Freeze!"

And then the muscular man they'd met earlier —Berg—popped out from behind a giant (and disgustingly realistic) replica of the human brain. His sleeveless T-shirt and acid-washed jeans had been replaced by a blue police-style uniform that looked two sizes too small. In fact, his clothes looked likely to burst if he so much as lifted a bulging arm over his head.

"Dang," Berg said when he was close enough to realize he was talking to the four kids. "It's just you

again."

"Sorry," Nick told him. "But I'm sure you'll catch some real punks one day."

"Oh, I will," Berg said. His expression turned wistful and his gaze drifted off to a spot about three feet above their heads. "I will."

Then with a rough jerk of the head, he shook the dreamy look off his face.

"Anyway, what are you doing out here?"

"Uhh," said Nick.

"Ohh," said DeMarco.

"Oooh," said Silas.

"We were just wondering where Ms. Wharton-Wheeler's office is," Tesla said.

The boys gaped at her in surprise. It hadn't occurred to them to tell Berg the truth. Or part of it at least.

"We wanted to ask her what museums were like in the old days," said Tesla. "You know, before they got so 'X-Treme.'"

"Well, her office is back in there," Berg said, nodding toward a small doorway in the nearest wall. "In that maze, with all the other administrative offices. But you won't find her there. She spends all her time puttering around with her baby."

"She has a baby?" Silas asked.

"I mean, she's working in her new exhibit. Up there." Berg pointed up the stairs. "It used to be *Going with Your Gut: A Journey through the Digestive System*, but she's replacing it with something else. About time, too." Berg shivered. "You've never experienced creepy till you've been alone on patrol in a giant colon."

"Um, yeah, I bet," Tesla said. "Well, thanks for the information. Come on, guys. We'll just pop in on Ms. Wharton-Wheeler and—"

Berg stepped in front of Tesla and put up his hands.

"Whoa, whoa, whoa! Those day passes of yours mean that you can be in the museum, but you can't just go wandering around wherever you want. Stick close to your uncle. I'll let Ms. Wharton-Wheeler know you want to talk to her the next time I see her."

"Gee, thanks," Tesla said.

"No prob, little missy. Keep your noses clean, kids."

As he walked off, Berg pulled out a flashlight, switched it on, and swung the beam this way and that as if expecting to find "punks" lurking behind every display case.

"Great," Nick sighed as he watched the guard walk away. "What do we do now?"

"Are you kidding? It's obvious," Tesla said. "We know Ms. Wharton-Wheeler went out to lunch and we know where she's been spending all her time when she's here. Which means we know where we should be going right now."

Tesla gave her brother a wide-eyed look that meant "Work it out."

It took him about two seconds. It would have

been one second, but he disliked the answer so much he thought it through a second time just to be sure.

"You think we should be going to the very place the security guard just ordered us not to go," he said.

Tesla shrugged.

"I prefer to look at it less as an order and more like a suggestion."

"Which you want us to disregard," said Nick.

Tesla ignored that comment, too. "The challenge," she said, tapping a finger against her lower lip, "will be avoiding getting trapped inside when Ms. Wharton-Wheeler comes back."

"Getting trapped inside what?" Silas said. "You guys lost me after 'What do we do now?'"

DeMarco pointed at the closed exhibit on the second level.

"Tez wants us to sneak in there and try to find out what that crabby curator lady's been up to."

Tesla nodded approvingly. "Very good." She grabbed DeMarco by the wrist and yanked his arm down to his side. "But maybe we shouldn't be pointing . . . ?"

She jerked her head to the left.

In the dark distance on the other side of the

dinosaurs, a little circle of light bounced here and there. They watched as it landed on a pair of human and chimpanzee skeletons in a glass case.

"All right, punks! Freeze!" Berg's voice echoed through the atrium. The light lingered on the skeletons a little longer.

Then a much quieter "Dang."

"Right," DeMarco said. "Sorry."

"I see what you mean about getting trapped," Nick said to Tesla. "If we're all up there in the exhibit, we won't see Ms. Wharton-Wheeler come back until she's in there with us. And even if we have a lookout on the balcony, he won't be able to see her come into the atrium. The entrance is right below the balcony and around a corner."

"You can see all the entrances from right here, though," DeMarco pointed out. "Maybe we have one lookout up on the balcony and another down here."

"But then what's the lookout supposed to do if he sees something?" Nick asked. "He can't go shouting 'Hey! Look out!' without giving himself away. And it's so dark in here that if he doesn't shout, whoever's watching from up there probably won't notice him."

"Then why not use the darkness to our advantage?" Tesla asked. She nodded again at the beam from Berg's flashlight, which was slowly working its way down one of the darkened corridors that branched off the atrium. "I mean, look how easy it is to see where that guy is. Light—that's the answer."

"I don't get that answer," Silas said.

"She's talking about having our lookout use light to let us know if someone's coming," Nick explained. "But where's the light gonna come from, Tez? We don't have a flashlight. Is the lookout supposed to start a bonfire? Set off fireworks? Turn on the Bat—?"

Nick's words trailed off and he turned away, suddenly lost in thought.

"Turn on the bat?" said Silas.

"Now *I* don't get it," said DeMarco.

Nick pointed at the entrance to the Hall of Genius.

"The stars that Copernicus and Galileo and Kepler are looking at in there. They're light-emitting diodes. LEDs," he said. "There must be some spares somewhere. All we'd have to do is figure out how to power one and we'd have our own—"

"Bat Signal!" Silas blurted out.

"I love it!" said Tesla, grinning. And with that she darted toward the doors leading back to the Hall of Genius.

Though usually Nick instinctively followed his sister when she rushed off on this or that mission, this time he lingered behind in the shadowy atrium, looking morose.

"What's the matter?" DeMarco asked him. "You figured out how to do it!"

"Yeah," Nick said. "But I forgot I didn't really want to do it in the first place."

SUPER-CYBORG GADGET GLOVE

FINGER #1 (INDEX FINGER): THE NICK SIGNAL

THE STUFF

- A comfortable, not-too-tight, not-too-bulky glove (see note below)

- 1 10-mm ultra-high-brightness white LED bulb (Radio Shack item #3125355)

- 1 CR2032 3-volt button battery

- Hot-glue gun

- 6 inches (15 cm) of 24-gauge solid speaker wire (you'll need more for other projects, so buy a roll)

- Scissors

- Wire strippers

- Electrical tape

Note: You should carefully choose the glove that will act as the base for your super-cyborg gadget glove. It should be comfortable and allow you to easily move your fingers. A larger glove will give you plenty of space to attach all your gadgetry, so try one that's a little bit big for your hand. Choose a glove that isn't too thick, and avoid one made from fuzzy fabric such as wool or fleece; the fuzz will make it harder for the wires to make contact. Be sure to check with your parents before gluing wires, batteries, and other stuff onto anything from your family glove drawer!

THE SETUP

1. The speaker wire consists of two joined plastic-coated strands. Pull the strands apart so that you end up with two plastic-coated wires.

2. Remove the plastic coating from the end of one of the wire strands, leaving enough bare wire to make a loop around the thumb of the glove (probably about 2 inches [5 cm]).

3. Loop the bare wire around the tip of the glove's thumb (check the length while wearing the glove to make sure the loop is big enough) and twist the end around the wire to secure it. Hot-glue the wire to the glove in a few spots to secure it.

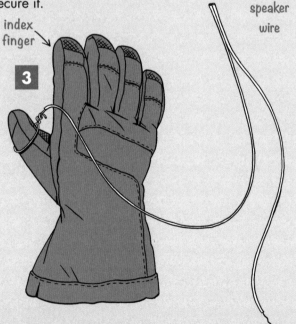

index finger

speaker wire

3

4. Run the plastic-covered part of the wire down the outside of the thumb toward the wrist and cut it so that it ends near the wrist. Remove about ½ inch (1.25 cm) of the plastic coating from free cut end. Hot-glue the wire in place somewhere on the side of the thumb.

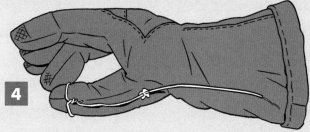

5. Take the other strand of separated speaker wire from step 1 and remove about 1 inch (2.5 cm) of the plastic coating from one end. Bend the bare wire over the glove's index finger so that the free end is on the underside of the finger. Poke the end of the bare wire into the glove to help secure it; glue some of the plastic-covered wire to the glove fingertip. (Don't cover the bare wire.)

6. Bend the free length of this wire so that it runs down the back of the index finger. Cut it so that it ends at the base of the finger. Remove about ½ inch (1.25 cm) of the plastic from the free end.

THE FINAL STEPS

1. Place the LED on the index finger on the knuckle closest to the hand, facing the fingertip. Twist the free end of the wire attached to the index finger around the longer (positive) LED wire.

2. Cut a piece of leftover separated speaker wire that is long enough to reach from the LED to the free end of the wire attached to the thumb. Remove about ¾ inch (2 cm) of plastic from each end of this wire.

3. Place the short (negative) wire of the LED on the top (negative side) of the battery. Place one end of the free wire that you just cut underneath the battery against the bottom (positive side). Wrap electrical tape around the LED's negative wire, the battery, and the end of the free wire. Leave the other (positive) LED wire (that you connected to the index finger wire in step 1) outside the tape.

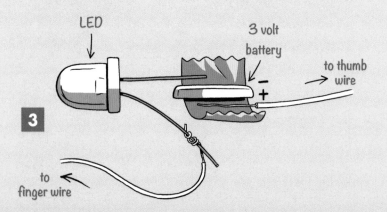

LED

3 volt battery

to thumb wire

3

to finger wire

4. Adjust the LED so that it points forward when you bring together the tips of your thumb and index finger. Secure the light to the index finger by wrapping electrical tape around the battery and LED connections and around the whole finger. Keep the positive LED wire from touching the battery.

5. Twist the remaining free wire end around the free end of the thumb wire. Cover all twisted-together wires with electrical tape.

6. To activate the Nick Signal, touch the tip of your thumb to the tip of your index finger so that the bare wires connect. When the wires make contact, you complete an electrical circuit, which powers the light.

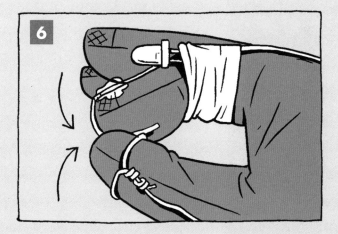

It was Silas who came up with the glove idea.

Nick and Tesla were tinkering with an LED and battery their uncle had found for them, trying to figure out how to hold the objects together, when Silas pointed at what looked like a loose flap of skin lying atop a toolbox nearby. It was actually a flesh-colored latex glove that Hiroko had brought in to slip over one of Plato's hands. (The rest of the animatronic looked fine, but for some reason the Greek philosopher's right hand was a ghastly sort of orange, as if he'd left it in a tanning bed about two hours too long. Replacing the new hand would have taken too much time, so Hiroko opted for a shortcut.)

"Why not glue the light and the battery onto that?" Silas said. "Then the lookout could just wear it. It'd be like something Iron Man would have. Except, you know. Not iron."

Nick and Tesla looked at each other in amazement.

"That's actually a good idea," said Nick.

"I know," said Tesla. "Except the latex probably wouldn't be strong enough, and it might react with the glue."

Nick and Tesla had been working on the floor in the Hall of Genius, near Plato's feet. Tesla crawled over to the toolkit, opened the lid, and began rooting through it. She pulled out a screwdriver, a monkey wrench, a soldering iron, two highlighter markers, a yo-yo, a scorched smoke detector, a stuffed (fake) rat (they hoped), and a half-eaten submarine sandwich. This being her uncle's toolbox, none of the contents came as a surprise to Tesla. Until something spoke.

"Hello! I'm Alan Turing!" said a man's voice with a clearly bogus British accent. "I'm the genius who laid the groundwork for the modern computer by blah blah blah yada yada yada et cetera et cetera. Li li li la la la and so forth. How long will this keep recording, I wonder?"

Tesla dug deeper into the toolbox and discovered that the voice was coming from a small metallic disk at the bottom. Several identical disks were scattered around it.

The voice did more *li li li la la la*-ing before abruptly cutting off.

"Uncle Newt," Tesla said, "was that you?"

Uncle Newt and Hiroko were working hard to get Darwin's newly reattached head to turn to the left, toward a giant Galapagos iguana, instead of spinning in circles atop its neck as it had been for the last ten minutes.

"Yeah," Uncle Newt said. "I did some experimenting with recordable sound chips. Thought we might wire them onto some of the animatronic figures so we wouldn't have to run all the sound files through the museum's network. The chips have memory for only about 30 seconds of sound, though, which wouldn't be enough. And the sound quality wasn't up to snuff, either. Or so some people insisted."

"It sounded like you were standing in a cave with a pillow over your face," Hiroko said. "And you can't imitate an English accent."

"Says who? Pip, pip, cheerio and—darn it, Darwin! You keep messing everything up!"

Darwin's head had come loose again.

Tesla went back to searching the toolkit and quickly found what she was looking for: a pair of dark work gloves.

Half an hour later, one of the gloves had a battery and LED attached to it.

"Aww," Silas groaned as Tesla flicked the light on and off. "It would've been way cooler with that skin-looking glove. As if the light was built right into your hand, like you were a mandroid."

"Cyborg," DeMarco corrected.

"Whatever," Silas said.

"The important thing is that it works," Tesla said. "Now we just have to hope Ms. Wharton-Wheeler takes really long lunch breaks."

"Yeah," said DeMarco. "It'd stink if we spent all this time making a gadget glove to signal that she was back from lunch and it turned out she was back from lunch already."

Tesla took off the glove and started walking toward the lobby.

"Well, there's only one way to find out if she's back, right?" she asked.

Silas and DeMarco followed her.

Nick gulped, and *then* followed.

At first it looked as if Uncle Newt and Hiroko were so busy with Darwin that they might not even notice the kids were leaving. But just as Tesla reached the big white partitions at the entrance, Hiroko called out to them.

"Where are you going this time?" she asked.

"We want to test the range of the signal glove we just made," Tesla said.

She held up the glove and gave the LED a couple quick flashes.

Hiroko looked at Uncle Newt, obviously deferring to him. Nick and Tesla were his responsibility, after all. Would he just let them and their friends amble off unsupervised?

Uncle Newt threw a quick glance at the glove.

"Cool!" he said.

Then he got back to work on Darwin's rotating head.

That's one silver lining when your Mom and Dad dis-appear, thought Nick. *You're constantly worried about them, but, man, you sure do get away with a lot.*

Back in the museum's big, gloomy lobby atrium, Tesla handed out the assignments. She and Nick would sneak into Ellen Wharton-Wheeler's second-floor exhibit because they were more likely to spot evidence of high-tech sabotage. DeMarco would stand guard on the balcony outside the exhibit because he was small and quick and less likely to be spotted by anyone—a roaming guard, say—down on the first level. And Silas would be the first-floor lookout, watching for Wharton-Wheeler while stationed outside the Hall of Genius, because that meant he wouldn't have to go anywhere and therefore couldn't get lost. (Tesla didn't mention that last reason out loud, but Nick figured it out.)

"Excellent!" Silas said. "So that means I'm the one with the cyborg gadget glove! Gimme, gimme!"

"Okay, okay. Just be careful with it," Tesla said as she handed it over. Until that moment, she hadn't considered what might happen to the glove if Silas were the one using it. She tried not to think about what his enthusiasm might mean for all the careful wiring they'd just done. "You saw how to turn the light on and off, right?" she asked.

"Yeah, yeah, yeah. I saw."

Silas tugged the glove onto his hand. He brought his thumb and index finger together, completing the electrical circuit that lit up the LED.

"E.T., phone hoooooome," he croaked, poking the glowing finger at DeMarco.

"What are you talking about?" DeMarco said, swatting Silas's hand away.

"You've never seen *E.T.*? What's wrong with you, man? It's a classic."

"Silas," Tesla hissed. "*Turn off that light before someone spots it.*"

"Right. Of course. Sorry."

Silas separated his thumb and finger, and the LED went dark.

"Don't turn it on again unless you see something, understand?" Tesla said.

"We should have a system for the signal. Like Morse code," Nick suggested. "Maybe a short flash and a long flash if Ms. Wharton-Wheeler comes in, but two shorts and a long if Berg or one of the other security guards is heading up the stairs to the second level. And how about two longs and a short if someone else comes along and . . . oh, forget it."

Silas had stopped listening and was once again aiming the lit-up LED at DeMarco.

"*P-shew! P-shew!*" Silas said, making the internationally recognized sound for "I'm shooting you with a ray gun." "Don't make me mad, dude," he said. "I've got a laser on my hand. Oooh! That could be my superhero name. Laserhand! *P-shew!*"

Tesla stepped between Silas and DeMarco.

"If you see someone coming our way," she said to Silas slowly, between gritted teeth, "make—lots—of—blinkies—with—the—pretty—light. Okay?"

"Lots of blinkies. Got it."

"Wonderful," said Tesla with a tight smile.

She turned to her brother and muttered, "Let's go, before I kill him."

"Good idea."

And off they went.

As Tesla, Nick, and DeMarco headed for the staircase that led to the second level, they passed near the other closed wing on the first floor. Unlike the partitions at the entrance to the Hall of Genius, these tall white doors were shut tightly.

From somewhere on the other side of the doors came the sound of voices and whirring, whining machines.

"You know what I think is back there?" Tesla said, keeping her voice low. "A you-know-what."

"I bet you're right," DeMarco agreed.

"Don't get too curious—the you-know-what has nothing to do with sabotage in the Hall of Genius," Nick warned them. "Just hope the doors to Ms. Wharton-Wheeler's exhibit aren't totally closed like those are."

And they weren't. When Tesla, Nick, and DeMarco reached the curator's wing on the second level, they found a gap between the partitions that was just big enough for them to slip through.

Before passing through, however, the kids crouched outside the doors and listened. They didn't hear a thing. And when they cautiously peeped their heads into the exhibit, there wasn't much to see, either. It looked a lot like the lobby: dim lights, dark shapes, deep shadows.

And no movement. No people.

Or at least none that they could see.

"Well, I guess we're going in," Tesla said. "Watch out for Ms. Wharton-Wheeler, DeMarco. And that Berg guy. If he thinks you are a punk, there's no telling what he might do."

"Don't worry about me," DeMarco said with a smile. "How much trouble could I get into in a museum?"

Tesla smiled back.

Nick grimaced.

"How much trouble could I get into in a museum?" was what DeMarco had said to his mother that morning when he was trying to talk her into letting him spend the day at the Learnasium.

DeMarco's mom thought it was dangerous for her son to be hanging around with Nick and Tesla Holt. And Nick was starting to worry that she was right.

"If you hear me, come out of there right away," said DeMarco. "There should be time for us to duck around that corner down the hall before Ms. Wheelton-Warner—"

"Wharton-Wheeler," Tesla corrected him.

"—before she gets to the top of the steps."

"Yeah," said Nick. "Except, around that corner is a dead end. If Ms. Wharton-Wheeler decides to go down the hall instead of into the exhibit, we're trapped."

"Maybe there's another exit," Tesla said to her brother. "Come on."

One at a time, they tiptoed through the doorway and into the darkness.

Silas, meanwhile, was feeling a little creeped out.

His friends were gone and he was alone in a big, murky, nearly deserted building. Plus he was standing beside a giant brain. A foam-rubber brain, sure, but a giant brain nonetheless. An evil brain, if Silas were to guess.

Silas would eat this stuff up if it was in a movie or a comic book or a game or a story his dad was telling. But in real life? Somehow it wasn't as much fun.

He squinted up at the balcony on the other side of the lobby. DeMarco was supposed to be up there watching, waiting for his signal. But if DeMarco was there, he was doing a great job of being sneaky because Silas couldn't see him at all.

Silas wanted desperately to activate the LED on the gadget glove. It would be the perfect distraction for a twelve-year-old boy waiting by himself in the dark. But he didn't—he knew what Tesla would do to him if he turned on the light at the wrong time. Or at least he could guess what she'd do, and his guesses were pretty disturbing. Besides, his friends were counting on him to signal properly so that they could escape. So he had to come up with something else to keep his mind occupied while he kept watch.

Silas looked at the glove. He made a dramatic gesture, pointing into the atrium's darkness and thinking, *Beware, criminals. You face the power of Laserhand!*

Then he decided that Laserhand needed a theme song.

"Laserhand. Laserhand. Does the cool stuff a laser can," Silas sang softly. "He melts steel. Blows up . . . uhh . . . wheels. Cuts through walls. Zaps . . . umm . . . malls. Ugh." He realized that theme songs were harder to write than he thought.

He started over.

"Laserhand. Laserhand. Does the cool stuff a laser can. He blasts crooks. Something ooks. Really cooks? Makes stuff fry. Bad guys cry. Look out! Here comes Laser-eep!"

Silas spun around.

Something was moving. He'd glimpsed it behind him, on the other side of the big brain.

He stopped and listened. There it was again.

Shuffling feet. Heavy breathing.

Getting louder. Coming closer.

Suddenly Silas wished he'd paid attention when Nick started babbling about Morse code. What was the signal for "HELP!!!"?

And then a shape lurched out from behind the brain.

For a sliver of a second, Silas thought, *Please be Berg. Please say "All right, punk!" Please be Berg. Please.*

But the shape didn't say "All right, punk." It definitely was not Berg. It was taller and broader than Berg. And of course, Berg didn't have a beak and clawed feet and dark wings that spread wide when he swooped down on his prey.

But this thing did.

DeMarco was in position on the terrace, watching for the distant pinprick of light from below that would mean "Get out of there!" He could tell where the giant brain was, but he couldn't quite see Silas. It was too dark. Yet from time to time, DeMarco would catch a dim flutter of movement that he assumed was his friend.

And then, something strange—was that *two* flutters, close together? And did he hear something echoing from across the vast hall? A gasp? A cry of surprise? The sound was too faint to be sure.

DeMarco squinted, leaning over the railing and trying to get a better view. He watched and watched for the flash of light that would tell him trouble was coming, that something was wrong and he had to warn the others. But all he saw were shadows.

"Did you hear something?" said Nick.

Tesla stopped and cocked her head. She seemed to be listening.

"Yeah," she said after a moment of complete silence. "The *tick-tick-tick* of wasted time."

She headed deeper into the dimly lit exhibit.

Nick frowned. He lingered where he was, still listening for noises from outside. He could've sworn he'd heard a faint, distant yelp. But he didn't hear anything now. Maybe it had just been his common sense saying "What are you doing? You don't know this

Wharton-Wheeler lady is up to anything. And this is, like, trespassing!"

"Come on!" Tesla called to him.

Sometimes it seemed to Nick that Tesla spoke a lot louder than common sense.

And so Nick followed.

The first part of the exhibit was a corridor lined with signs and pictures, but it was almost too dark to see them. From the detail that was visible, it was obvious that the exhibit featured some kind of space theme. Nick recognized a famous photograph of Robert H. Goddard standing beside one of his early liquid-fueled rockets, and a little farther were images of the Soviet *Sputnik* satellite and Yuri Gagarin, the first human to reach space.

Tesla was as nuts about space exploration as Nick was—it was a love they'd both inherited from their space-obsessed dad—yet she didn't slow down to admire the pictures or try to read the signs. Even when they reached the end of the corridor and the true scope of the exhibit became obvious, Tesla kept hurrying onward while Nick stopped to say "Whoa."

To his left was what looked like a NASA mission control center. To his right was a life-size re-creation of the *Apollo 11* moon landing. Above him hung a model of the ISS, the International Space Station, spanning thirty feet across. And straight ahead was, well, *more.* There was so much, it was hard to take it all in.

Which is maybe why Tesla wasn't even trying. She just swept past displays with headings like "There's Gold in Them Thar Asteroids" and "The Case for Space: Colonization," two subjects that normally would have stopped her in her tracks.

"Keep your eye out for a hidden back exit, like the one in the Hall of Genius," Tesla said. "We may need it if Ms. Wharton-Wheeler comes back while we're still in here. And look for anything that seems out of place. A coffee mug or a water bottle or a laptop. That'll be where she's been working."

"Yeah. Got it. Will do," Nick muttered halfheartedly.

But he was thinking that it was hard to keep looking for things that were out of place when the things that were *in* place were so very cool.

There was a hand-cranked wheel loaded with beanbag astronauts to demonstrate how centrifugal force could simulate gravity on a spaceship. There was a "Star Bar" where you could buy samples of the same dehydrated juice and chocolate milk served on the ISS. There was even a kid-size space suit, which was slit up the back so that kids could climb into it. Nick was tempted to give it a try, not only because he'd always wanted to put on a space suit but also because it seemed like a great place to hide.

"You see anything?" Tesla asked him.

"Oh, yeah!" Nick said, the marvel clear in his voice.

"I mean *clues*."

"Oh. Right. Nah."

Tesla gave her brother a sympathetic look.

"Look, Nick, I feel the same way you do," she said. "From what Ms. Wharton-Wheeler said about the Hall of Genius, I was expecting her exhibit to be a real snooze. 'The Wonderful World of Cement' or 'An Interactive History of Library Dust' or something. But this is pretty amazing. We'll have to come back when the X-Treme Learnasium is open to the public again. Then we can take our time and see everything. Okay?"

"Assuming they'll let us out of jail for a trip to the museum," Nick grumbled.

"Oh, come on. No one's going to send a couple kids to jail for trespassing."

Tesla paused to push down on a small water-bed-like display that demonstrated how a warp drive might create bubbles in spacetime to move ships faster than the speed of light. A tennis ball rode the resulting ripples from one side to the other.

"If we're caught, we'll probably just go to juvenile hall," Tesla said, watching the tennis ball. "And maybe get placed in a foster home."

"Not funny, Tez."

"Who says I was joking?"

"Well, then, let's get out of—hey."

"Hey?"

Tesla turned to look back at her brother.

He was standing in front of a display labeled "The Case for Space: Power."

"Tez, you *gotta* come check this out," he said. "It's about space-based solar power. And there's something funky about it."

Tesla headed his way. Fast.

They had been reading everything available about space-based solar power for the past week—ever since a mysterious friend of their parents told them that space-based power is what their mom and dad had been working on when they disappeared. Not soybean irrigation in Uzbekistan, as Nick and Tesla had been told.

The display demonstrated how space-based solar power would work. In a glass case was a blocky gray grid and, about a foot away from it, a tambourine attached to a rod. The grid, as the sign nearby explained, emitted ultrasonic sound—sound with a frequency above a human's range of hearing. Even though people couldn't hear the sound, they could see its effect. When the emitter was switched on, ultrasonic sound waves would hit the tambourine and cause it to vibrate. In a similar way, a satellite could beam the energy it collected from the sun to cities on Earth. That energy would be not sound waves but microwaves, but the principle was similar.

Nick read aloud from the sign under the display. "The possibility of the wireless transmission of power," he recited, "was first championed by Nikola Tesla, who—"

He had to stop because the text after that was covered by duct tape. Just as it was on Tesla's sign in the Hall of Genius.

His sister reached out for the tape.

Nick grabbed her hand.

"Wait," he said.

"I know, I know," she said. "If we can't get the tape back on right, Ms. Wharton-Wheeler will know someone's been here."

"It's not that. I thought I heard something."

"Again?"

Tesla sighed and listened, too.

And this time she definitely heard something. A distant muffled . . . flapping?

That definitely wasn't DeMarco calling to them to run for it. But it was a reminder of what they were supposed to be doing.

"We've only got time for one mystery at the moment," Nick said to Tesla. "This can wait."

Tesla turned and hurried off, once again scanning the exhibit for proof that Ellen Wharton-Wheeler was a saboteur.

Nick stayed in place, listening intently. What *was* that noise?

It must be something innocuous, something he could ignore, he assured himself, because Silas and DeMarco were out there. All they had to do was wait,

and watch, and Nick and Tesla would know if there was a *real* reason to worry.

How could such a simple plan possibly go wrong?

"Or how about this?" the giant dancing owl said to Silas. "I moonwalk, segue into the cabbage patch, then throw in some twerking, and climax with a head spin."

The owl went gliding backward a few feet and

then began hopping from one clawed foot to the other as its wings flapped back and forth.

"Well? Huh? Whaddaya think?" the owl panted as he skidded to a stop. "Better than the electric slide? Or should I go back to doing the robot?"

"Uhh . . . that's good," Silas said to him. Which is what he'd said about the electric slide and the robot, too. And the humpty dance, and Gangnam style before that. But this big dumb bird wouldn't stop dancing.

Five minutes earlier, the owl had burst out of the darkness, jumping at Silas and saying, "Hey! A kid! Just what I need!"

Silas's understandable response: "Whaaa!"

"Sorry, kid! Didn't mean to scare you," the owl said to him. "I wasn't expecting to see you, either. I thought I'd be in here working on my moves all alone. But then I heard your singing."

"Y-your m-m-m-moves?" Silas said.

Once Silas realized the giant owl was just a guy in a goofy suit, he calmed down and found it a little easier to speak. After all, how many owls—even giant ones—wear sunglasses, backward-facing baseball caps, and droopy jeans with their underwear showing? Before noticing all that, Silas had thought he was about to be carried off to a nest and snarfed down like a big squirrel.

"Yeah, my moves," the owl said. "I'm Coolicious McBrainy, the X-Treme Learnasium's new extreme mascot. I'm going to be at the museum every day showing youngsters that science and technology can be totally rad!"

"How are you gonna do that?"

The owl shrugged. "Dance routines, mostly. And a little improvised mime comedy. Speaking of which . . ."

At that moment Coolicious McBrainy leaned forward and began walking, taking exaggerated steps that led him nowhere.

"Uhh, do you need help?" Silas asked.

"No! I'm walking against the wind. It's a mime classic. All right, forget that. Tell me how this looks."

The owl-man wiggled his tail feathers, rolled his wings in big circles, and swayed from side to side.

"It's so hard to tell what a move looks like when you're inside a new suit," he said. "Can you tell I'm doing the hustle?"

"What's the hustle?"

Coolicious McBrainy immediately stopped moving

and stood with shoulders slumped.

"Ugh. Okay. How about this?" He began riding an invisible horse while waving one wing over his head. "You recognize this move, don't ya?"

"I'm sorry," Silas said, "But could we do this later? I'm a little busy right now."

The owl stopped dancing and stared at Silas with owl fake eyes the size of dinner plates.

"Doing what?"

Silas considered the two possible answers:

(A) "Being a lookout for my friends, who are sneaking around in one of the exhibits even though a security guard told them to stay here."

(B) "Oh, nothin'."

He went with B. Which was how he ended up spending the next few minutes trying to be a lookout for his friends while simultaneously critiquing the dance steps of a six-foot-tall owl.

"Maybe you should try a few spearoettes," Silas said eventually. He didn't know anything about dancing; he was just trying to find something to say, because standing there watching the owl dance was starting to weird him out big time.

"You mean pirouettes? Like in ballet?" Coolicious

McBrainy asked. "In an owl suit?"

Silas nodded. "Or jazz hands," he added. "You can never go wrong with jazz hands." Silas brought up his hands and waved them in the air. Then he waved them like he just didn't care. "Er, well, I guess jazz *wings*, in your case."

The owl's big, bulbous upper body rocked from side to side. The man inside the costume was shaking his head.

"You're not getting it, kid." the owl told Silas. "I'm trying to reach your generation. Get down with the youth, you feel me? Somehow I don't think jazz hands are going to . . . hey. What's with the glove?"

"Huh?"

Coolicious pointed a wingtip at the gadget glove on Silas's right hand.

"You're wearing one glove. Is that some kind of fashion thing?"

"Oh. Yeah. A fashion thing. Exactly. All the kids are doing it."

"It's the first time I've seen it."

Silas gulped. "All the *fashionable* kids, I mean," he said.

Coolicious put his wings on his hips.

"And *you're* one of the fashionable kids?"

Aside from the glove, Silas was wearing dirty jeans and tattered sneakers and a faded *Star Wars* T-shirt that didn't quite cover his belly. "Totally fashionable," Silas answered. He nodded rapidly. If he could keep the owl talking, maybe he wouldn't dance anymore. "Now," Silas said, "the move you really need to work into your routine is the—*eep*!"

"The eep? I don't know that one. I sure am learning a lot today!" Coolicious said.

But Silas wasn't listening. He was staring, horrified, at a distant figure walking past the gift shop; it was about to turn a corner and start up the broad marble steps that led to the museum's second level.

It was the figure of Ellen Wharton-Wheeler.

Silas had missed her when she first came inside because he was too busy watching an owl do the cha-cha slide. Now he had only seconds to send the warning signal to DeMarco.

But first he had to distract Coolicious, and fast.

"Look!" Silas said. "An eagle!" He pointed at a spot behind the owl about fifty feet above their heads.

Coolicious turned to look. "What do you mean?" he said. "Like, flying around in here?"

Silas turned on the LED at his fingertip. Wasn't there some kind of code he should be flashing? Long light, short light? Long light, long light, short light? Short light, long light, short light? He couldn't remember.

Whatever. He just waved the light in the air and hoped for the best.

"I don't see anything," Coolicious said.

Silas turned off the LED just as Coolicious turned to look at him, and then he pointed into space again.

"No, wait. It's a bat!"

"Really?"

Coolicious turned around again.

Silas relit his finger light and stuck his hand straight up.

Ellen Wharton-Wheeler was halfway up the stairway. A dozen more steps and a turn to the left and she'd be at the doors to her exhibit—and De-Marco and Nick and Tesla would be in real trouble if they didn't get out of there fast.

"This stupid mask," Coolicious said. "I can't see five feet in front of me. Is the bat—whoa! Is your finger glowing?"

The big owl had turned back around while Silas

was watching Wharton-Wheeler.

"Yeah," Silas said, trying to laugh it off. "It glows," he said. "It's, uh, another fashion thing."

He switched off the LED. If DeMarco hadn't seen the signal by now, it wouldn't matter. He and Nick and Tesla were about to get caught, and there was nothing more Silas could do about it.

"So, anyway," he said to Coolicious, "have you thought about doing the Dougie?"

"Finally!" Tesla announced triumphantly.

"Did you find something?" Nick called to her from the other side of the space exhibit.

"Yeah! Come check it out! By the moon rover!"

Nick hurried to join his sister. She was standing by what looked like a dune buggy with a satellite dish sticking out of the hood. It was a model of the lunar rover that had been used by astronauts on the *Apollo* missions to the moon. Lying on one of the rover's seats were a coffee mug, an appointment book, and a binder packed with papers. Near these objects, built into the dashboard beside the steering wheel, were a telephone, a computer screen, and a keyboard.

It was the control panel for the exhibit, hidden in plain sight just like the one in the Hall of Genius. Only here the screen wasn't displaying the exhibit controls. Before going to lunch, Wharton-Wheeler had been checking her e-mail.

"All right, we found where she's been working," Nick said. "Now what?"

"Now we do a thorough search of—"

"Nick! Tesla!" DeMarco hissed from the entrance. "She's coming!"

"You've got to be kidding me," Tesla groaned.

"Silas gave the signal," DeMarco went on. "Get out of there. *Now.* Do you hear me?"

"We hear you," Nick said. He took his sister by the arm. "Don't we, Tez?"

"But—but—"

Nick started to pull his sister away from the screen.

Tesla yanked her arm loose. "I just need a few seconds to—hey!"

Something Tesla saw on the computer screen made her eyes go wide.

"We don't have a few seconds," Nick said, latching on again and tugging her away. "We never found a back exit. We've gotta go out the front—where Ms. Wharton-Wheeler will be coming in!"

Tesla tried to break free, but this time Nick held on tight.

"Come on, Tez," he said. "We can't stop the sabotage from juvenile hall, can we?"

"Okay, okay. You're right."

Tesla stopped resisting and started running alongside her brother. But a part of her wanted to turn around and head straight back to the control panel.

She'd gotten just half a second's peek at the screen, and a message in the e-mail inbox had caught her eye. It was from Katherine Mavis, the X-Treme Learnasium's executive director. All Tesla had been able to see was the subject line:

RE: DESTROYING THE MUSEUM FROM WITHIN

When Nick and Tesla stepped out of the space exhibit, DeMarco was nowhere in sight. What they could see was the top of Ellen Wharton-Wheeler's head as she came up the staircase.

One more step and she'd see them. There was no time to escape around the corner, and no place to hide.

Nick grabbed Tesla again and spun her around so that she was looking back the way they'd just come.

"Oh, Ms. Wharton-Wheeeeee-lerrrrrr!" he called out loudly, peering through the gap in the tall white partitions blocking off the exhibit. "Yoo-hooooooo! Are you in there?"

"I'm back here," came the curator's voice behind them. "What are *you* doing here?"

Nick and Tesla turned to look at her with (they hoped) convincing looks of surprise.

"Why, we're looking for you," Nick said innocently. "Didn't Berg tell you?"

"Who?"

"Berg. You know. The security guy who's all hulked out?" Nick said.

Wharton-Wheeler cocked an eyebrow but said nothing. She'd stopped a few feet away, and she was so tall that Nick had to bend backward a little bit to look up into her eyes. It made her seem even more intimidating—as if she was glaring down at him from a throne . . . or a judge's bench.

"Anyway," Nick continued, his voice cracking, "Berg said he'd let you know we wanted to talk to you. But, well, I guess we got a little antsy, so we decided to find you ourselves."

"Why would you want to talk to *me*?" Wharton-Wheeler asked.

"Well, uh, we wanted to apologize again for the head in the refrigerator."

"And we were curious about the you-know-what," Tesla threw in.

Wharton-Wheeler scowled at her.

"The what?"

"The big secret whatever in that other new wing downstairs."

Wharton-Wheeler smiled politely but said nothing. But her silence did say something: Tesla had guessed right. The you-know-what *was* in the new wing downstairs.

"We've got a theory about it," Tesla continued.

"You do?" Wharton-Wheeler said.

Nick turned to look at his sister in a way that said "We do?"

"It's got something to do with Nikola Tesla," Tesla said.

Wharton-Wheeler looked both surprised and impressed. But certainly not friendly.

"That part of the museum is not my concern anymore," she said. "Like that tourist trap sideshow attraction your uncle's working on. I've got just my little corner here to do with as I think best. Speaking of which, I have work to do."

And with that she stepped forward.

Nick stepped aside.

Tesla did not.

"We couldn't resist a peek at your exhibit," she said. "What's it about?"

Wharton-Wheeler paused.

"It's called *Whatever Happened to the Final Frontier?*" she said. "It covers the history of space exploration and the reasons our country should recommit itself to it."

"Cool!" Nick said.

"I like it," Tesla said.

Their obvious sincerity warmed the curator a bit.

"Thank you," she said. "I like to think it turned out well."

"Could we go in and look around?" Tesla asked.

Wharton-Wheeler immediately cooled right back down.

"You're welcome to come back once the X-Treme Learnasium is open for business," she said, her voice dripping with scorn as she pronounced the museum's new name.

She then stepped around Tesla and slipped

through the gap in the partitions.

"For now, you two should stay with your uncle and his friend," she said. "This is no place for curious children."

She took hold of the big white doors from the inside and slammed them shut in Nick and Tesla's faces.

A moment later, Nick and Tesla were heading down to the first floor.

"Hey! Wait up!" someone said behind them.

DeMarco came hurrying down the steps to join them.

"Did you make it around the corner?" Tesla asked him.

"Naw. *Somebody* waited too long to give us the signal. After I warned you guys, I managed to duck behind one of those big nasty organs. I think it was a kidney. Or maybe a liver. Anyway, I heard your conversation with Ms. Wheeler-Wharton."

"Wharton-Wheeler," Tesla corrected.

"Right. Good job talking your way out of trouble.

If you're gonna get caught, that's the way to do it. So was it worth it?"

"No," said Nick.

"Yes," said Tesla. And she proceeded to tell Nick and DeMarco about the e-mail subject line she'd seen.

"Regarding destroying the museum from within? On an e-mail from that Katherine Mavis lady, the museum director?" Nick said. "That doesn't make any sense. Why would she and the head curator want to destroy their own museum?"

"Ms. Wharton-Wheeler obviously hates the new direction it's gone in—all the 'X-Treme' stuff," Tesla pointed out. "As for Ms. Mavis, I don't know . . . but I sure want to find out."

DeMarco grinned. Nick did not.

They both knew what was in store for them all: more risky snooping.

DeMarco was neutral on snooping, but he loved taking risks.

Nick didn't like either.

They found Silas still waiting by the big brain. He was trying to teach himself how to moonwalk.

"Why were you so late with the signal?" DeMarco

asked. "By the time you flashed your little light, Ms. Wha-Whee was halfway up the stairs."

"Sorry. I got distracted by Coolicious McBrainy."

"Who?" Nick, Tesla, and DeMarco all said at the same time.

"He's an owl," Silas explained, still trying to glide backward but just scuffing the floor. "And, I have to admit, a really good dancer."

Nick, Tesla, and DeMarco were all speechless at the same time.

"He left just a second ago," Silas went on. He bumped into the brain, spun around, and started dancing in the opposite direction. "Said he had to go to the staff changing room and adjust his costume."

"Ahhh. *Costume*," DeMarco said, sounding relieved. "I was starting to worry about you, dude."

"I'm still confused," said Nick. "Why is there a guy walking around the museum in an owl costume?"

"He's the Learnasium's new mascot. He got here early to warm up for the big opening whoop-de-doo tonight." Silas finally stopped moonwalking and gave his friends his full attention. "So what happened up there, anyway?"

"Later," Tesla said, heading for the Hall of Genius.

"Right now we need to talk to Uncle Newt and Hiroko."

But Uncle Newt and Hiroko did not want to talk to them.

"Do you realize how much we still have to do?" Uncle Newt asked as he struggled to straighten Charles Darwin's nose, which had been knocked sideways the last time the scientist's head fell off. "Hiroko and I still have to get Isaac Asimov back on his feet, strengthen Louis Pasteur's grip so he won't throw any more beakers, retest Nikola Tesla's head—"

"I just noticed one of Jane Goodall's chimpanzees lost an arm," said Hiroko, who was on her hands and knees looking for an eyeball that had popped out of Aristotle. "And something went wrong with Henry Ford's back. He looks like the hunchback of Notre Dame."

"Great. So we've got to rearm a chimpanzee and reback Henry Ford." Uncle Newt stopped twisting Darwin's nose and thought for a moment. "Although maybe we should leave Ford as he is. I never liked that guy."

Uncle Newt took a step back and considered Darwin's nose, which was still so crooked it looked like the naturalist had been punched by a prizefighter. "Good enough! Next!" Uncle Newt hustled over to the jungle scene that Jane Goodall shared with Dian Fossey and began literally beating the bushes looking for the chimp's loose arm.

"I just had a few questions about Katherine Mavis," Tesla said.

"Don't really know her! Talks a lot of gibberish! Just happy she called! Eureka!" Uncle Newt said.

He pulled out a hairy black appendage from under a fake fern and then started looking around for the ape it belonged to.

"Why *did* she call you?" Tesla asked. "I mean, I know you're a genius and all, but how'd she find out about you?"

"Mark Carstairs! Original designer! Worked together once! Recommended me! Eureka again!"

Uncle Newt squatted down beside an animatronic chimp and began examining a silver rod jutting from its shoulder.

"Can you think of any reason Ms. Mavis might

have to—"

"Tesla!" Uncle Newt said. "Getting clue? Speaking loudly in incomplete sentences! Stressed! Busy! Later!"

"Okay, I'm sorry. Just one more question," Tesla said. "Where is Ms. Mavis's office?"

Uncle Newt waved the chimp arm at Einstein's chalkboard and the exit hidden behind it.

"Right, left, right, right," he said.

"No," Hiroko said. "Right, right, left, right."

"No. It is definitely right, right, left, left," said Uncle Newt.

"That's not even what you just said," Hiroko told him.

"It's not?" Uncle Newt scratched his head with the monkey's paw. "Well, anyway, it's definitely turn, turn, turn, turn. You can't miss it!"

They missed it.

The kids found a broom closet, various storage rooms, and even the staff workout room. But they couldn't find the office of Katherine Mavis, the

X-Treme Learnasium's executive director—and, as Tesla kept saying, its executive traitor.

Then Nick heard a vaguely familiar voice echoing down one of the museum's seemingly infinite hallways.

"We're ska-funk-punk-emo-metal with a retro grunge twist," the voice was saying. "And I rap."

The kids followed the sound to a door in a dead-end hall. When they peeked in, they saw a scruffy-looking man with thick glasses and gelled hair that stood on end like a little patch of black grass. He was sitting at a clutter-covered desk, his back to the door, holding a cell phone in one hand and a bag of potato chips in the other.

"Hey," DeMarco whispered, "it's the computer guy."

"Senior system manager," corrected Nick.

"Yeah. The monkey T-shirt dude," said Silas. "Hobo."

"Mojo," said Tesla. "Mojo Jones."

"I sent you a link to our website. Did you get it?" Mojo was saying into his phone between bites of potato chips. "Oh. Okay. Yeah, I'm sure you get a lot of e-mails like that. But you really ought to take mine out of your spam folder and check it out because you haven't heard a band that rocks harder than—hello? Hello?"

He tossed his phone onto the desk.

"Jerk," he sighed.

Tesla cleared her throat.

Mojo slapped his hands on his computer keyboard and began typing furiously. The bag of chips fell to the floor.

"Work-work-work, code-code-code," he started saying, fingers flying across the keys. Then he swiveled in his chair to face the doorway. "Oh, hi, kids. How can I help you?"

"We're trying to find Katherine Mavis's office," Tesla said.

"You're almost there. A right, a right, and a left. It's with all the other administrative offices. You can't miss it."

"Wanna bet?" said DeMarco.

"I know you're busy, Mr. Jones," Tesla said quickly. "But can I ask you something?"

"Well . . . ," Mr. Jones said, finally halting his banging on the keyboard. "I guess I could spare a few seconds." With his left foot, he carefully shoved the potato chip bag under his desk.

"Thanks," Tesla said. "I'm just curious. The computer controls for the animatronics in the Hall of Genius—how complicated are they?"

"Not very. I've tried to make all the interfaces pretty idiot-proof."

"So just about anybody could change the settings or whatever?"

"I suppose, as long as you had the right log-ins. Is your uncle having trouble again?"

"No, no, he's fine," Tesla said. "Thanks."

"Can I ask a question?" said Nick.

"Sure," Mojo said with only the slightest hint of exasperation.

"Your boss, Ms. Mavis, uh . . ."

Nick scrunched up his face and rolled his hands in the air as he fought to find the right words.

". . . umm . . . hmm . . ."

"Yeah?" Mojo said.

"Well . . . what's her deal?" Nick said finally.

Mojo shrugged.

"Her deal? I don't know. She was brought in to shake things up at the museum, and that's what she did. Before coming here, she was head of marketing over at the San Francisco Scientastic Explorezone. There's always been a big rivalry between them and us, so it was kind of like having the quarterback of the 49ers come in and, uh, do plays for the, uh, whoever the 49ers fans don't like. Sorry. I knew I shouldn't try to make a sports analogy."

"That's okay. I get it," Nick said. "She used to play for the other team."

He gave his sister a significant look.

Motive? it said.

"Can I ask a question?" DeMarco said.

Mojo winced. For a half second, he looked like he was in pain.

"Sure," he said through gritted teeth. "What do I have to do today, anyway? It's not like we have a massive rededication ceremony in"—he checked the time on his computer screen—"four hours and forty-four minutes."

DeMarco ignored the sarcasm and pointed at the words on the man's T-shirt.

"What's a Migraine Monkey Missile Test?"

And in that instant, Mojo Jones's demeanor changed completely. He went from being an irritated sourpuss to a beaming, grinning, excited puppy.

"That's my band!" he said. "We're a ska-funk-punk-emo-metal-grunge power trio. With rapping. I'm the front man. We've been trying to get established. Get some gigs, you know? It's tough, though. The ska-funk-punk-emo-metal scene isn't what it used to be, and the grunge thing throws some people off. And not everybody's into my rapping. Sooner or later, we're gonna get noticed, though. It's just a matter of making a splash at the right moment. We've been working on a video, but we ran out of . . . well . . ."

Mojo's smile had begun to fade, but with a wave of his hands it came back full force.

"Never mind that. Gotta keep it positive, right? That's our plan. Keep on rockin', build word of mouth, and then conquer the world. And you guys can help!"

He yanked open one of the desk drawers, and started pulling out Migraine Monkey Missile Test CDs, T-shirts, posters, and bumper stickers. Then he jumped up from his chair and started handing them out to the kids.

"Here you go," he said. "Enjoy! And don't forget to follow us on Twitter and like us on Facebook and review us on iTunes and Amazon."

He paused for a moment while adding a Migraine

Monkey Missile Test refrigerator magnet to the pile Silas was already holding.

"What's with the glove?" he asked.

Silas had refused to take off the gadget glove even though it wasn't needed anymore for signaling.

"I'm a cyborg!" he said, lighting up his finger.

"That's *cyborg*," DeMarco corrected. "No, wait, you got it right."

"Uh, okey-dokey," Mojo said and dropped the magnet onto Silas's pile, taking a big step backward. "Well, I guess I'd better get back to work. Thanks for dropping by."

He closed the door to his office.

Then the kids heard a loud *click* as he locked it.

"Thanks, Silas," Nick grumbled. "Now he thinks we're nuts."

"Yeah, thanks," said Tesla. Unlike her brother, she sounded like she meant it. "I was afraid he was going to start rapping. Anyway, how'd he say to get to Ms. Mavis's office? Right, left, right?"

Nick shook his head.

"Left, right, right."

"No," said DeMarco. "Left, left, right."

Tesla slumped and turned to Silas.

"Go ahead. You may as well say it," she told him.

"Say what?"

"How do *you* think Mr. Jones told us to go?"

"Well, I'm pretty sure he said right, right, right, right."

"Of course you are," Tesla said, heaving a resigned sigh. "Fine. Let's just start walking. We're bound to get somewhere eventually."

She was right. There were more wrong turns, but once Nick started leaving Migraine Monkey Missile Test merchandise behind like a trail of bread crumbs, they at least stopped doubling back on themselves.

After several long minutes of wandering, they finally ended up in a corridor lined with offices and work cubicles.

Here, at last, the museum seemed alive. A dozen people in business clothes were talking loudly and quickly on phones, scurrying here and there with paperwork, chattering at each other over cubicle walls. Every conversation seemed to be about the same thing: the museum's reopening gala.

The kids got a few curious looks, but the day passes hanging around their necks seemed to do the trick and the looks never turned into stares. The only person who talked to them was a middle-aged man who glanced up from his work, smirked at the CDs and T-shirts they were still carrying, and said, "So Mojo got to you, too, huh?"

A Migraine Monkey Missile Test calendar hung on the wall behind him.

A few seconds later, they finally passed Katherine Mavis's office. The door was open, and they could see the director sitting at her desk. She seemed a bit young to be in charge of a museum—there wasn't even a wisp of gray in her blonde hair—but she was most definitely head honcho. As the kids watched, she was simultaneously chewing out someone on the phone, pounding out an e-mail, and eating ramen noodles out of a plastic cup.

"What do you mean Channel 5 isn't sending a camera crew?" she barked, sending a chunky mist of half-chewed noodles spraying over her computer. "You told me you could leverage major media, maybe take us viral, and so far all we've got confirmed for coverage are a couple local newspapers and a lousy NPR station! The opening of a Trader Joe's gets more traction!"

She noticed the kids peeking in at her, flashed them an unconvincing here-and-gone smile, and waved.

The kids waved back and then darted off around the nearest corner.

"We've got to get her out of there so we can get a look at her message to Ms. Wharton-Wheeler," Tesla said once they had reached a safe distance.

"I don't know if that's such a great idea, Tez," Nick said.

"Yeah. What about all those other people back there?" said DeMarco. "I think they're gonna notice if we just barge into their boss's office and start fooling around on her computer."

Tesla nodded. "You're right," she said.

Nick looked relieved.

"We've got to get *all* of them out of there."

Nick looked horrified.

"How are we going to get a dozen people to leave their offices all at once?" DeMarco asked.

"Free food!" said Silas.

Tesla shook her head. "Nah. What are we supposed to do? Bake 'em a cake?"

"Stink bombs!" said Silas.

Tesla kept shaking her head. "Which we're going to get where?" she said.

"Fire alarm!" said Silas.

Tesla suddenly stopped shaking her head.

"No, Tez," said Nick. "Setting off a fire alarm when there's not a fire is illegal and unsafe and immoral and . . . just no. No, no, no, no, no."

"Don't worry. I know how wrong it would be to set off a fire alarm," said Tesla.

She smiled in a way that told Nick he'd won the battle but lost the war. Then she added: "That's why we're going to build our own alarm."

SUPER-CYBORG GADGET GLOVE

FINGER #2 (MIDDLE FINGER):

TESLA'S FALSE-ALARM ALARM

THE STUFF

- Your gadget glove (you know—the one with the signal light on it!)

- 1 battery-operated buzzer/alarm (we suggest a 90dB Piezo Pulse, Radio Shack item #2062399)

- Wire strippers

- Scissors

- A finger's length of 24-gauge solid speaker wire

- 1 9-volt battery

- 1 9-volt battery connector

- Hot-glue gun

- Electrical tape

THE SETUP

1. Wire the middle finger of the glove using a single strand of separated speaker wire, following the same technique as for the index finger (see page 65): Remove about 1 inch (2 cm) of the plastic coating from one end of the speaker wire. Bend the bare wire over the glove's middle finger so that the free end is on the underside of the finger. Poke the end of the wire into the glove to help secure it and then glue it to the glove fingertip. Bend the free length of wire so that it runs down the back of the middle finger. Cut it at the base of the finger. Trim ½ inch (1.25 cm) of the plastic from the free end.

2. Hot-glue the buzzer onto the back of the glove.

3. Cut the middle finger wire and the black wire from the buzzer to length so that they meet. Remove about ½ inch (1.25 cm) of the plastic coating from the buzzer wire and twist the wires together.

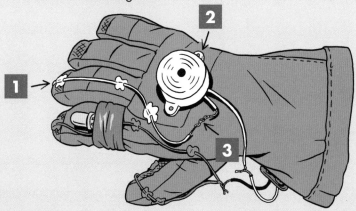

4. Hot-glue the 9-volt battery to the underside of the glove wrist.

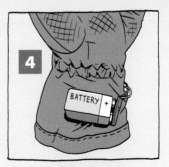

5. Attach the 9-volt battery connector to the battery.

6. Connect the battery connector's red wire to the buzzer's red wire.

7. Connect the black battery wire to the thumb wire (see page 67).

THE FINAL STEPS

1. Cover the twisted wires with electrical tape.

2. To sound the alarm, touch your middle fingertip to the thumb tip. The alarm will sound for as long as the wires touch.

CHAPTER

8

The kids were back in the Hall of Genius. Tesla had noticed a smoke detector in her uncle's toolbox earlier that day. It was the kind you'd find in most homes—a thick white plastic disk—except that half of it was scorched black and one side seemed to be slightly melted.

"Uncle Newt," Tesla said as she pulled it out, "why do you have a smoke detector in your toolbox?"

Uncle Newt was standing behind Henry Ford with his arms wrapped around the animatronic figure's chest. He was trying to straighten Ford's back, but it looked like he was giving the inventor the Heimlich maneuver.

"I've worked at places where safety protocols weren't up to my standards, so I bring backup," he said.

"*You* have safety standards?" Nick said. He'd once seen his uncle ignore a fire that was spreading up his lab coat because he didn't want to stop an experiment. "I can't take my eye off this test tube," Uncle Newt had said. "Why don't you just throw a bucket of water on me or something?"

Tesla turned over the smoke detector. The power light was off.

"Does this thing even work?" she asked.

"Come to think of it, I'm not sure," Uncle Newt said. "The last time I used it, I blew the place up."

"Man," Silas said with a laugh, "remind me never to go to work with you!"

"Silas," DeMarco said, "we *are* at work with him."

"Oh, yeah." Silas stopped laughing. He looked around at the various arms and hands and heads still scattered around the Hall of Genius. "Remind me never to do it again."

Tesla took out a screwdriver from the toolbox

and opened the smoke detector's battery compartment.

It was empty.

So much for her uncle's high safety standards.

"Would you mind if we took this apart?" Tesla asked her uncle. "We'll get you a new one. *With* a battery."

"Sure. Fine. Go for it."

Uncle Newt tightened his grip on Henry Ford's chest and pulled. The figure straightened to its full height and then, as Uncle Newt let go, quickly doubled over at the waist, arms flopping to the floor.

"Wonderful," Uncle Newt said with a sigh. "Now he's doing yoga."

"I'll be over to help you in a second," Hiroko told him. She was scrolling through the exhibit's computer controls, looking for glitches. She wasn't finding any.

Next, she turned to look at the kids.

"I'm sorry you're all stuck here while we have to keep working. I hope you're finding ways to amuse yourselves."

"Don't worry," Tesla said. She started trying to pry apart the smoke detector. "We are."

Nick was nearby, leaning against Sigmund Freud's chair.

"I think you and I define 'amuse' differently," he said to his sister.

Tesla just smiled as the top of the smoke detector popped off in her hands.

Despite Nick's reluctance, he helped his sister remove the alarm horn—a round component about the size of a quarter—from the smoke detector. Silas and DeMarco hovered nearby, watching.

"Now what?" Silas asked.

"We connect this horn to the power source and wiring we've already got *handy*, so to speak," Tesla said.

She looked at the gadget glove, which was still on Silas's hand.

Silas grinned. "Excellent," he said, holding out his hand as if he expected Tesla to slip the alarm horn on it like a ring. "Do it!"

"You're going to have to take off the glove, Silas," Nick told him.

Silas snatched his hand back.

"What? No! It feels like a part of me now. I don't know if I *can* take it off."

"Silas, I have a plan," Tesla said, keeping her voice low so that Uncle Newt and Hiroko wouldn't hear. "And for it to work, the person using the alarm—and the glove—needs to be the quickest one, the quietest one, and the best hider. Do you think that's you?"

"Umm . . . yes?" Silas said.

Nick, Tesla, and DeMarco shook their heads incredulously. Silas outweighed each of them by at least thirty pounds.

"Okay," Silas finally said. "You win."

Slowly, reluctantly, he peeled off the glove.

"I'm gonna miss being a cyborg," he said.

Ten minutes later, the new and improved gadget glove was ready. Maybe.

"Hey, guys," Tesla said to Uncle Newt and Hiroko. "There might be a little beep in a second. It's just us, okay?"

Hiroko was still hunched over the controls.

"Sure," she said.

Uncle Newt just gave a thumbs-up sign without looking away from the bent spectacles he was trying to put back on the face of Carl Jung.

Tesla moved the thumb of the glove toward the alarm-horn wire on the middle finger. The wires connected and . . .

A sudden screeching *NEEEEEEEEEEEEEEEEEEE* made everyone jump.

Tesla released the connection, and the alarm horn went silent.

"Well, that definitely works," Nick said, rubbing his ringing ears.

"Why do you need your glove to beep?" Uncle Newt asked as he bent down to retrieve Jung's eyeglasses, which in a moment of synchronicity had flown out of his fingers when the alarm went off.

"It's a long story," Tesla said.

She was hoping her uncle was too busy to want to hear it, and she was right. He simply went back to fumbling with the Swiss psychiatrist's glasses.

"So," said DeMarco, "the quickest, quietest, and most daring of us gets to wear the glove."

"Who said anything about most daring?" Nick asked.

"Oh, I added that because I know who Tesla was talking about." DeMarco smiled smugly. "Me. Right,

Tez?"

"But *I* can be quick and quiet and daring," Silas whined.

He was staring at the glove so intently that Tesla almost expected him to call it "my precious" and try to snatch it away.

"You have an important role to play, too," she told Silas.

"I do?"

"Absolutely! Quick—nod your head and say um-hmm."

Silas nodded his head and said "um-hmm."

"Wow! Perfect!" Tesla exclaimed.

Silas brightened a bit.

"So what's my job?" Nick asked.

"That depends," Tesla said. "Do you want to distract or snoop?"

"What if I don't want to do either?"

"Then we'll have to let Silas do all the talking."

"Um-hmm," Silas said, nodding. "Um-hmm. Um-hmm."

He was practicing.

"Fine," said Nick. "I'll distract."

"And I'll snoop," said Tesla. "I'll explain on the

way back to Ms. Mavis's office."

She passed the gadget glove to DeMarco and then started walking toward the rear exit hidden behind the Einstein display.

Suddenly she came to a stop in front of Nikola Tesla.

"What is it, Tez?" asked Silas, who'd been following so closely he almost marched right over her when she stopped.

Tesla was looking at the biography of her namesake—and in particular at the part covered with duct tape.

She reached out and started to pick at one corner of the tape. When she'd peeled up enough, she pinched it and started to pull.

"Tesla?" Hiroko said. "Is there something wrong over there?"

"No," Tesla said, quickly smoothing the tape again. "I'm just wondering why part of the Nikola Tesla sign is covered up."

"I've wondered about that, too," Hiroko said. "All I know is that Katherine Mavis asked us not to remove that tape, so I haven't even taken a peek. You know, out of respect to the museum. We are basically guests here."

Hiroko cocked an eyebrow at Tesla.

Tesla tried to smile at her.

"Sure! Absolutely! Couldn't agree more! Well, come on, guys. Let's go get those Migraine Monkey Missile Test CDs that DeMarco wanted for his sisters."

"Huh?" Silas said.

Tesla grabbed him by the arm and pulled him toward the exit.

"Hiroko's starting to wonder what we're up to," she said once they were all in the corridor.

"Why don't we just tell her about the e-mail message you saw?" Nick asked.

"Because if she doesn't believe us, we'll get sent home for sneaking around," Tesla said. "And if she *does* believe us, we'll get sent home to keep us safe from the saboteurs. Either way, we lose. Now come on. I'm starting to get the hang of these hallways."

Tesla turned right and started walking.

"I don't know," she heard her brother mutter behind her. "What's so bad about being sent home where it's safe?"

He did have a good point.

Which is why Tesla ignored it.

Nick and Silas walked past one work cubicle after another, looking lost. Fortunately, the museum's employees were still too busy to pay much attention to them.

"I think the restroom's this way," Nick said, just in case anyone was listening.

Silas nodded. "Um-hmm," he said.

Finally, they reached Katherine Mavis's office. The door was still open, and once again the director was simultaneously typing and talking on the phone.

"No shrimp puffs *or* mini quiches? Are you not conceptualizing what I'm telling you?" she barked. "We've been forward-promoting this infoccasion for months! You do know we've confirmed some C-list celebrities for tonight, don't you? Maybe even a B-minus or two? Well, you don't transition those affluentials into donors by serving pigs-in-blankets and potato chips! This is a major soirée, not a PTA meeting! I need you to value-add these hors d'oeuvres right now because I have zero cycles for this. JDI!"

"Hey," Nick said loudly. "Do you hear something?"

"Um-hmm," Silas said, nodding.

A high-pitched whine was echoing from the hallways ahead of them.

NEEEEEEEEEEEEEEEEEEEEEEEEEE.

"Hold on a sec," Mavis said, lowering her phone.

She cocked her head and listened for a moment.

One of the workers left his cubicle and poked his head into her office.

"Katherine," he said, "do you know what that noise is?"

"Proactive question, Matt. I was about to come out and ask you the same thing," she replied. "It sounds like some kind of alarm."

"It's not the fire alarm," the man named Matt said. "That makes more of a *BEEEEE-uhhhhh, BEEEEE-uhhhhh* sound."

Another worker popped out of her cube to join the conversation.

"And it's not the security alarm," she said. "That goes *whooooo-EEEEEE-chirp-chirp, whooooo-EEEEEE-chirp-chirp.*"

"That's a car alarm, Amy," Mavis said.

"Yeah," said Matt. "The security alarm goes *CHEEEEE-errrrrrr, CHEEEEE-errrrrrr*."

Amy shook her head skeptically.

"What's going on?" someone else said. It was Mojo Jones, the computer guy, hurrying up the hall to join the conversation.

"Hi, kids," he said when he noticed Nick and Silas. "Had a chance to listen to the CD I gave you yet?"

"Mojo, what's that noise?" Mavis said before the boys could answer. "Is it the security alarm?"

Mojo shook his head.

"The security alarm's more of a *CHEEEEE-ooooooooooh, CHEEEEE-ooooooooooh*."

"Told you," Matt said to Amy.

"You said *CHEEEEE-errrrrrr*," she shot back.

"Close enough!"

"Well, whatever it is," Nick said, "it's definitely *some* kind of alarm. Which means maybe we shouldn't just be standing here talking, right?"

Silas nodded and um-hmmed.

"They're right," Mojo said. "We should clear everyone out till we know what's going on."

The director groaned.

"I'll call you back," she said into the phone. "And

when I do, you'd better have some shrimp puffs! JDI!"

She down slammed the phone, typed something into her computer with hard angry jabs onto the keyboard, and then stood and stalked out of her office.

"JDI?" Nick asked.

"Just do it," Matt answered. "It's her mantra."

"Mantra?" Nick asked.

"Okay, people—listen up!" Mavis said. "The universe has decided that we're not stressed out enough today. So I'm going to have to ask all of you to put a pin in your current task and step outside while I lean in to this disturbance and see what this noise is about. Is that PAC?"

"That means perfectly absolutely clear," Matt said to Nick before he could ask. Mumbling and grumbling, the museum's staff filed out of their workspaces and began trudging off. Nick and Silas went with them, although they dropped back to the end of the line.

The hallway ended at a "T" intersection. The museum workers headed left, toward an exit sign and a metal door at the end of the corridor. Katherine Mavis turned right—toward the sound of the alarm.

Mojo followed. "I'll tag along, just in case," he said. "It doesn't sound like a computer or network problem, but you never know."

"Thanks, Mojo. At least somebody around here isn't totally acluistic." She peered down the hallway, missing the total confusion that her remark brought to Mojo's face.

Nick and Silas paused to watch them go.

"Be careful!" Nick called out.

Mojo glanced back over his shoulder.

"Don't worry guys," he said with a smile. "We'll be fine."

But Nick hadn't been yelling to him.

DeMarco was peeping around a corner, waiting to see who might come hurrying up the hall to investigate the *NEEEEEEEEEEEEEEEEE* that had been deafening him for what seemed like an hour (but was really more like a few minutes). Even though he held the gadget glove as far from his body as he could, the thing was *loud*. Why oh why, he wondered, did he have to be the quickest, the quietest, the bravest, the coolest of his friends? Sometimes it was a real pain.

DeMarco had to admit, though—part of him was kind of enjoying the suspense. He'd always thought of being a stuntman or a race car driver or something like that when he grew up. But this skulking-around, about-to-be-chased thing had possibilities. Maybe he could rent himself out to jaded billionaire playboys who wanted to experience the thrill of hunting human quarry. Hunting with paintball guns, of course. DeMarco craved excitement, but he wasn't crazy.

Yeah, he imagined . . . *DeMarco Davison, Prey for Pay*. That had a nice ring to it. The only challenge would be finding the jaded billionaire playboys. He knew they had to be out there somewhere, but he'd never run across any personally. Maybe he'd ask Nick and Tesla. They attracted strange and dangerous people like honey attracted—

DeMarco shook off his Prey for Pay daydream. He'd become used to the sound of the gadget glove alarm, but a shout had cut through the shrill whine. The voice was familiar—it was Nick's—but the words were garbled.

Had he yelled "Big awful!"?

"Beak airful!"?

Wait . . . "Be careful!" Yes, that was it.

DeMarco saw a pair of shadows stretched from around the corner he'd been watching. In about half a second, at least two people would be following them.

It had definitely been "Be careful!"

DeMarco and his friends had been getting lost in the museum's labyrinthine hallways all day. But now they could make the maze work for them, so long as he was fast enough and no one walked up behind him. DeMarco spun on his heel and dashed for the next corner. He rounded it, stopped, and peeked out again, looking for the shadows. He realized how lucky he was that not all the lights in this part of the museum had been turned on, which meant that people cast shadows. And as soon as he saw them, he took off again.

Two more sprints around two more corners. That was all Tesla had asked him to do. Then he'd duck into one of the museum's many storage rooms and turn off the alarm. Hopefully, that would give Tesla enough time to get the goods on Mavis and Wharton-Wheeler. If not, well, it meant that DeMarco had worked up a lot of adrenaline for nothing.

Good thing I love adrenaline, DeMarco told himself.

The shadows appeared again.

DeMarco turned and ran.

Tesla heard the blare of the alarm horn fade into the distance.

DeMarco was on the move. Which meant it was time for her to move, too. Fast.

She stepped out of the bathroom she'd been hiding in and darted into Katherine Mavis's office. Hopefully, it would take only a moment to call up the e-mail and find her message to the curator. If everything went smoothly, she might even have time to print it out.

Tesla sat in the director's chair and spun around to face the computer on the desk.

A rectangular box hovered in the middle of the screen. In it were four words.

```
MUSEUM-NET LOG-IN
ID:
PASSWORD:
```

The director had logged off her computer before leaving her office.

Tesla was foiled! Thwarted! And furious, too, because she hated when that happened.

"No way! No way, no way, no way!" she ranted. "An alarm goes off and you take the time to log off your computer? What are you, lady? Paranoid?"

Of course, Tesla realized, it wasn't paranoia if Ms. Mavis really did have incriminating e-mails on her computer. It was smart.

Tesla kicked herself—literally, banging her right foot into her left shin—for not seeing this turn of events coming. Still, maybe all was not lost. Maybe she could find something that would make all the preparation and risk worth it.

She began scanning the desk for clues, with no idea what those might be. A copy of *Sabotage for Dummies*? A voodoo doll in the shape of the museum with pins stuck in it? A to-do list with "Destroy Hall of Genius" written between "Buy eggs" and "Pick up dry cleaning"?

Then an old-fashioned date-book planner caught her eye. It was lying next to the desk phone, open to the calendar for the week. Tesla pulled it over to her and reviewed the schedule written on it.

The woman was certainly busy, she had to admit. Practically every day of the week was jammed with conference calls, interviews, meetings during breakfast, lunch, and dinner. And the rededication ceremony that night. Of course.

But then Tesla spied a note scribbled in the slot for 4:30 p.m.: "W-W, meeting room 2."

Bingo!

"W-W" obviously wasn't Wonder Woman. Or Willy Wonka. Or Where's Waldo. There could be only one person at the museum with those initials.

So, Tesla thought, *Ms. Mavis and Ms. Wharton-Wheeler are getting together to plot face-to-face, eh?* Smart again. There'd be no electronic trail to follow, no e-mails or texts or voice messages that someone could find. No evidence. Unless . . .

Tesla checked the old-fashioned analog clock that was hanging on the wall above the desk. There was no time to lose: the meeting was little more than an hour away. Tesla would have to hurry if she wanted to be ready for it.

She stood up and started for the door just as Berg, the burly security guard, stepped through it.

"Ms. Mavis," Berg said, "Have you heard an alar—huh?"

Once his surprise wore off, Tesla could tell he was tempted to call her a "punk."

But he managed to restrain himself.

"Hold it right there, *miss*," he said instead.

CHAPTER 9

Five minutes later, Tesla found herself sitting in an uncomfortable chair in the museum's security office. The room contained some filing cabinets, a bulletin board, a bank of flickering video monitors, a desk, and, sitting behind the desk, one very glum-looking man. He wore the same police-style uniform as Berg, but he looked older and flabbier. The nametag on his shirt said RUFFIN.

"Okay, Berg," Ruffin said with a sigh. "What is it this time?"

"I caught her creeping around Katherine Mavis's office," said

Berg, who was standing next to Tesla. He put a hand on her shoulder.

Tesla shrugged it off. "I wasn't creeping around," she said. "I was walking."

Ruffin glanced at the pass hanging around Tesla's neck. "You're one of the kids here with what's-his-face and what's-her-name? The animatronics geniuses?" He rolled his eyes as the last word left his lips.

"Yes," Tesla said. "What's-his-face is my uncle."

"So why did you go into our director's office?"

Tesla folded her arms across her chest.

"To sit in her chair," she said firmly.

"Sit in her chair?" said Ruffin.

Tesla nodded. "I look up to Ms. Mavis," she said. "A young woman like her in charge of a big, wonderful place like this? It's inspiring. I just wanted to feel what it was like to sit at her desk. You know, bask in her glory a minute. And I was just leaving when he walked in," Tesla said, jerking her thumb at the muscle-bound guard standing beside her. "Wasn't I?"

She turned to stare at Berg.

"Yes," he said with obvious reluctance.

"And I hadn't taken anything, had I?"

"No," Berg grated out.

"He made me turn out my pockets," Tesla explained to Ruffin. "The only thing in 'em was gum and lint."

"And money!" Berg added.

"My own money. Two pennies and a quarter," Tesla said to Ruffin. "If I was in there to steal stuff, I could have done a lot better than that."

"Young lady," Ruffin sighed after a moment, "I don't believe you meant to do anything wrong."

"Aww!" Berg whined.

"But you must have known you weren't supposed to go in any of the offices unattended," Ruffin continued. "That day pass you're wearing says we trust you, and you betrayed that trust, whether you meant to or not."

Tesla nodded and tried to look sheepish and contrite. It wasn't an expression she wore very often, so she wasn't sure if she was doing it right. Ruffin kept talking. Tesla tried to pay attention, but she'd noticed something on one of the video screens behind him: a room that Tesla didn't recognize. She could see displays along the walls and

Learnasium guards standing in each corner. In the middle of the room, a group of men and women were huddled over what looked like two pieces of machinery. Two of the men were wearing coveralls, and when Telsa squinted, she could read a logo printed on the back:

Abruptly, the logo—and everything around it—disappeared. Ruffin had turned around and switched off the monitor.

"Here I am about to let you off the hook," Ruffin said, "and you don't even have the courtesy to pay attention?"

"I'm sorry," Tesla said. "I just got distracted. I know what I did was wrong and rude and stupid, and I apologize. It won't happen again."

"Good," Ruffin said. "I have enough to worry about today without—yes?"

Katherine Mavis had appeared in the doorway, with Mojo Jones behind her. "Hi, Carl," Mavis said to Ruffin. "Quick Q&A: Did a security alarm go off a few minutes ago?"

"Oh, yeah! I forgot to tell you, Chief," Berg said. "An alarm went off a few minutes ago."

"Gee, thanks for the report, Berg," Ruffin said dryly. "What kind of alarm?"

Berg rubbed his chin.

"I don't know. It made sort of a *NEHHHHHHHH* sound."

"It was more of a *NEEEEEEEEEEEEEE*," said Mojo.

"That's not the security alarm. It goes *cheeeeeEEEEEE-ooooooooOOOOH*," Ruffin said. "And the fire alarm is *MEEEEE-uhhhhhh*. And anyway, I would've seen an alert on the network if any of our alarms went off."

"Maybe something in the system malfunctioned when we lost power earlier," Ms. Mavis suggested.

Ruffin shook his head.

"That wouldn't change a *cheeeeeeEEEEEE-ooooooooOOOOOH* to a *NEEEEEEEEEEEEE*."

"Well, we heard something, Carl," Mavis said. "And I don't want any *cheeeeeEEEEE-ooooooOOOOOH* or *NEEEEEEEE* when we're about to monetize a cohort of V.I.P. predonors in a couple hours. Why don't you lateralize some boots on the ground for a little due diligence?"

Tesla stifled a "Huh?"

Ruffin seemed to understand, though.

"Of course, Katherine," he said with a sigh. "Berg, go check it out."

Berg straightened to his full height—which wasn't quite to the director's shoulders—and looked like he wanted to salute.

"I'm on it, Chief! Ms. Mavis, why don't you show me where you think the *NEEEEEEEE* was coming from."

"It seemed to come and go. That was one of the weird things about it," Mavis said as she led Berg out of the office. "But the last time we heard it, we were up this way. Near the east exit."

Mojo stepped aside to let Mavis and Berg pass. Once they were beyond him, he leaned back into the security office.

"Everything all right?" he asked Tesla.

"Oh. Sure. Mr. Ruffin and I were just talking about . . . stuff."

"Hopefully you were telling him about your favorite new band."

Mojo pointed at the Migraine Monkey Missile Test logo on his T-shirt.

Tesla smiled apologetically.

"No. Sorry. I haven't had a chance to listen to your CD yet. I'm sure I'll be raving about it to everyone once I do."

"Well, you won't have to tell *me* about it," Ruffin said. "There's no one in the museum that Mojo hasn't given that CD to. It's actually not that bad, though I like the funk a lot more than the punk and all the rest of it."

"Ska-punk-emo-metal. With a retro grunge twist," Mojo said.

"And you rap," Ruffin said in a weary but indulgent way. "But much more important, you code. Which is what you're supposed to be doing right now so that we can tell our friends from *hmm-hmm-hmm* there won't be any more blackouts."

"This guy," Mojo said to Tesla, shaking his head and jerking his thumb at Ruffin. "You come to *work* and he actually expects you to work. It's nuts." He gave Tesla a grin and a wave. "Later."

And with that he left.

Ruffin obviously expected Tesla to do the same. He stared at her silently, eyebrows high on his forehead, with his hand held out toward the door.

"Our friends from *hmm-hmm-hmm?*" Tesla said to him.

His expression didn't change; his hand didn't move.

"I expect *me* to work, too," he said. "If people would only let me."

"Okay. I understand."

Tesla thanked him and walked out the door.

She did understand.

She had work to do, too.

No sooner had Tesla started down the hallway than she saw a giant owl rounding the corner at the other end. "Thanks," the big bird was saying to someone he'd left around the corner. "Have a think-tastic day!"

The man in the owl suit stopped when he

noticed Tesla coming his way. Tesla saw that he had a museum day pass hung around his neck. And there was a blue winter glove pinned to the end of one of his wings.

He did a spin and a split, then popped back up to his feet-slash-talons.

"How do you like my glove?" he asked Tesla.

"Um," she stammered. "It's . . . it's nice."

"I hear all the cool kids are wearing 'em these days."

"Oh. Yeah. Definitely."

"Excellent." The owl stuck his glove out to Tesla. "Coolicious McBrainy's the name, youth outreach is the game."

"Hi. I'm Tesla." She gripped the glove lightly to shake the owl's hand. Or wing? Feathers?

"You're not in trouble, are you?" Coolicious said, tilting his huge round head toward the security office.

"I just had some explaining to do," Tesla answered.

"Well, good, Tesla," Coolicious answered. "I'm sure everything will work out fine." He then proceeded to moonwalk away from her, waving good-bye with his gloved wing the whole time. Tesla waved back in a daze.

"Stay in school, Tesla," the owl called to her. "And have a think-tastic day!"

So Silas hadn't dreamed the giant dancing owl after all.

Usually Tesla was surprised when Silas turned out to be right about something. But this was the biggest shocker yet.

Tesla was getting better at navigating the museum's corridors. She'd gotten lost only once since leaving the security office, and she realized her mistake as soon as she saw the door marked STAFF LOCKER ROOM. She'd already passed the door four times that day, enough to know she'd taken a right when she should have gone left two corners back.

Just as she turned around, the door opened and Coolicious McBrainy stepped out.

Surprised to see the giant owl again so soon, Tesla stopped in her tracks. She expected him to break into some dance move. But Coolicious simply acknowledged her with a wave and then walked swiftly past.

Tesla shrugged and went on her way. But she couldn't shake the feeling there was something different about the owl, something she couldn't quite put her finger on. When she realized what it was, she turned and called, "Hey! You're not wearing your pass! Better put it on quick or else Berg's gonna slap you in handcuffs!"

Coolicious looked back just long enough to give her another wave. Which was when Tesla noticed something else: there was no glove on the end of his wing. He must have figured out that wearing a glove wasn't so cool after all.

Tesla watched as the owl turned sharply at the first corner and disappeared without a word. He'd been outgoing and friendly before, but now it was almost as if he was fleeing from her.

So much for "youth outreach."

It didn't really surprise Tesla, though. The kind of person who makes a living dressing as moon-walking wildlife, she reasoned, might be prone to mood swings.

Tesla hurried off to the rendezvous point with

the boys: the Hall of Genius.

Silas was studying the equation on Einstein's blackboard: $E = mc^2$.

"E equals mick two?" he said. "You know, I've seen this thing before but I never understood it."

"I don't know anyone who understands it," said DeMarco.

Nick was pacing nervously nearby. "E equals em cee squared," he said. "It means energy is equal to mass times the speed of light squared."

"Correction," DeMarco said. "I know one person who understands it."

Nick stopped pacing and started wringing his hands instead.

"No, you don't," he said. "I don't really get it either."

He was staring past the Einstein animatronic at the hidden exit door, which suddenly, finally, opened.

"Tesla! Where have you been? We thought you'd been—"

Nick caught himself just in time. He peeked back at Uncle Newt and Hiroko to see if they'd noticed.

They hadn't. They were too busy arguing about which head went on which Wright brother.

"Orville's the handsome one," said Hiroko.

"But this is the handsome one," Uncle Newt replied.

Nick turned back to his sister.

"We thought you'd been caught," he said in a whisper.

"I was," said Tesla.

And then she told them the story.

"All that," Nick groaned when she was done, "and we still don't have any proof."

"Not yet. But I can tell you when we should have some," Tesla said.

"A little after 4:30?" Nick guessed.

"Exactly." She crossed her arms, looking confident.

"We're gonna get proof at the meeting that Ms. Mavis and Ms. Whatever-Whatever are having?" DeMarco said. "How?"

Now Tesla slumped her shoulders, looking a

little deflated.

"I haven't figured out the how yet," she admitted.

Silas cleared his throat and took a step toward the Einstein animatronic.

"Allow me," he said.

He pried free the little piece of white chalk Einstein was holding and began drawing on the chalkboard. When he was finished, this is what he'd drawn:

"Glovey?" said DeMarco as Silas stepped back from his masterpiece.

Tesla plucked the chalk from Silas's hand.

"Hey! I wasn't done!" he said.

"Oh, you're done," Tesla told him. She wedged the chalk back into Einstein's animatronic fingers and then turned, picked up an eraser, and began wiping away Silas's diagram. "Before Uncle Newt and Hiroko get a look at it," she whispered.

"It's actually a pretty good idea," Nick said, "aside from the fact that we don't have a carrot, a rabbit, an eagle, or a webcam."

"Take away all those things, and what's left that's good?" Tesla asked.

Nick stepped up next to his sister and pointed at the one part of the plan she hadn't yet erased:

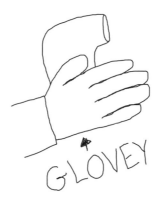

GLOVEY

"We might not have a webcam, but there's something else we could attach to the glove," Nick said.

He turned to look at Uncle Newt's toolbox sitting on the floor nearby.

Tesla followed his gaze. For a moment she racked her brain, trying to remember everything she'd seen in there earlier. What was it Nick thought they could use? The highlighter markers? The yo-yo? The stuffed rat? The submarine sandwich?

Then Tesla smiled.

"The sound chips," she said. "You're a genius!"

"Well . . . ," Nick said modestly.

But he didn't argue.

SUPER-CYBORG GADGET GLOVE

FINGER #3 (RING FINGER):

NICK'S HANDY ONE-HANDED RECORDER

THE STUFF

- Your gadget glove

- 1 digital sound recorder (9V Recording Module, Radio Shack item #2102855)

- Wire strippers

- 24-gauge solid speaker wire

- Scissors

- Hot-glue gun

- Electrical tape

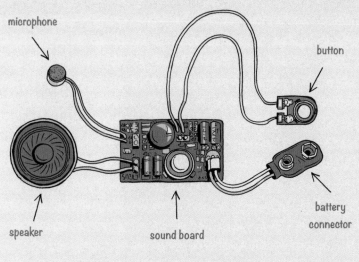

microphone

button

speaker

sound board

battery
connector

DIGITAL RECORDING MODULE

THE SETUP

1. Very carefully, cut the two wires that connect the button to the sound board. Cut halfway between the button and the sound board.

2. Very, very, very carefully, use the wire strippers to remove slightly less than ½ inch (1.25 cm) of plastic coating from the cut ends of the sound board wires.

3. Cut a 6-inch (15 cm) length of speaker cable (you can leave the strands attached if you like). Remove about ½ inch (1.25 cm) of plastic coating from one end of both strands and twist one strand onto each of the sound board wires. Each strand of the speaker wire should be attached to its own sound board wire.

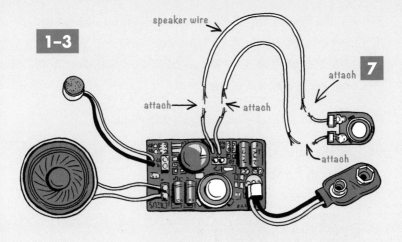

1–3

speaker wire

attach → 7

attach →   ← attach

attach

4. Wrap each pair of twisted wires securely with electrical tape.

5. Hot-glue the voice recorder securely onto the back of your gadget glove.

6. Carefully remove some plastic from the ends of the button wires you cut in step 1. Hot-glue the button onto the palm of the glove in a spot so that when you bend your ring finger, it naturally pushes the button.

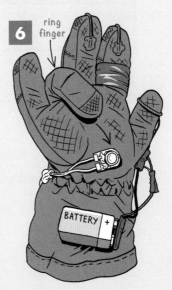

6   ring finger

BATTERY +

7. Cut the loose ends of the speaker wire from step 3 just long enough to reach the button on the palm. Strip the ends of both strands of the speaker wire and twist them onto the two button wires.

8. Wrap the twisted wires with electrical tape.

9. Use the scissors to snip the wires attaching the battery connector to the sound board.

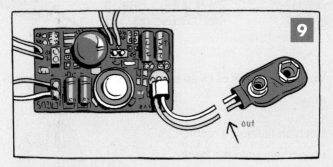

10. Connect the red wire from the sound recorder to the joining spot of the red wires from the False-Alarm Alarm (page 122, step 6).

11. Connect the black wire from the sound recorder to the joining spot of the thumb wires.

12. Tape the connected wires together with electrical tape.

THE FINAL STEPS

1. Hot-glue the microphone and speaker onto the glove wherever there's room. A good spot for the microphone is on top of the alarm buzzer.

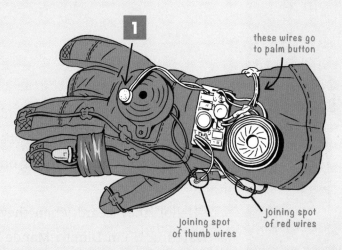

these wires go
to palm button

Joining spot
of red wires

Joining spot
of thumb wires

2. To activate the voice recorder, push and hold the palm button with your ring finger. The voice recorder should record for up to 20 seconds.

3. To play back the sound, press the button on the sound board.

The first sound chip that Nick and Tesla pulled out of Uncle Newt's toolbox already had a recording on it.

"Hello!" they heard when they activated it. "I em Dimitri Mendeleev and I em Russkie chemeest who inwent Periodic Table! I em tryink to do Russkie accent but I think I sound more like Dracula! Blah! I vant to drink your mercury and cesium!"

"As an actor, you make a great scientist," Hiroko said to Uncle Newt. They had finally reattached all the heads and appendages and props that had shaken loose earlier and were now trying to fix a rip in the fake bathtub "water" of the ancient Greek mathematician Archimedes.

"Thanks!" Uncle Newt chirped obliviously.

The next chip Nick and Tesla picked out hadn't been used for one of their uncle's sound checks. Which meant that it was ready to do some good old-fashioned bugging.

They brought it over to Einstein's blackboard and got set to attach it to the gadget glove.

"Hey," Nick said softly as they got to work, "what time is it, anyway? For all we know it's after 4:30 and we missed Ms. Mavis's meeting with Ms. Wharton-Wheeler."

"I'll go check."

Tesla stood and headed toward the control panel built into Sir Alexander Fleming's work table on the other side of the Hall of Genius.

"And you said Ms. Mavis wrote 'Meeting Room 2' in her planner, but we don't even know where that is," Nick added. He held up the sound chip. "This won't do us any good if we can't even find the room we need to put it in."

"I'll scout it out," said DeMarco, heading for the

exit.

"Me, too," said Silas.

"You know," Tesla said to her brother as their friends left, "you're really good at seeing why things *won't* work."

Nick shrugged. "It's a gift."

Tesla walked over to the computer to check the time, but on reaching it something else caught her eye. The control dashboard for the Hall of Genius was still on the screen, and she could see the username that Uncle Newt and Hiroko had used to log in: Carstairs1.

"Why are you guys logged in as Carstairs1?" Tesla said. "I thought Carstairs was the designer who got fired."

"We're using his old username and password," Hiroko said. "Mr. Jones was supposed to get us new ones, but he never got around to it. Too much going on this week, I guess."

"But doesn't that mean Carstairs could still— *yipe!*"

She finally noticed the time. They had less than half an hour to get the glove ready and find Meeting Room 2.

"Could Carstairs still yipe? I don't know," Uncle Newt said. "What's yiping?"

Tesla didn't answer. She was rushing back to Nick. "Work fast," she whispered. "It's already after four."

Nick looked up from the gadget glove.

"You know, even if we have this ready by 4:30, it won't do us any good if we can't figure out how to—"

"Forget your gift. Just *hurry*."

"Got it," he said.

He hurried.

DeMarco and Silas returned just as Nick finished adding the sound chip to the glove.

"We found the meeting room," DeMarco said. "There's a problem, though."

"Let me guess," said Nick. "Since the chip can record for only thirty seconds, we'll have to be listening to the conversation to know when Ms. Mavis and Ms. Wharton-Wheeler are saying something incriminating. But to do that, we'd have to be in the room with them, and there's no place to hide."

DeMarco's eyes widened.

"He's good," he said to Tesla.

"At seeing problems," Tesla said.

"Hey! I can see solutions, too!" Nick protested. "This was my plan, remember?"

Tesla picked up the gadget glove.

"All right," she said. "Let's go to Meeting Room 2 and see if you can save your plan."

"Hide under the table? That's your brilliant solution?" DeMarco said.

"Wow," said Silas, "I could've thought of that." Then he added, "Sorry, dude."

Nick gave them a listless, defeated shrug. "It's the best I can come up with," he said.

Meeting Room 2 was long and narrow, with one door, a rectangular boardroom-style table, and a dry-erase board mounted to the wall. There was no closet, no podium, nothing to hide in or behind.

"Well, I think hiding under the table could actually work," said Tesla.

"You do?" Silas and DeMarco said at the same

time.

"Yeah . . . you do?" said Nick.

Tesla nodded.

"The table's for, like, twenty people," she said. "It's huge. But there's only gonna be two people sitting at it. And it's obvious where they'll be." She pointed at one end of the table. "In the seats closest to the door. So someone hiding under the other end of the table should be fine."

"Unless that someone sneezes," said DeMarco.

"None of us has a cold," said Tesla.

"Or unless Ms. Wharton-Wheeler or Ms. Mavis drops a pen in the middle of the meeting," said Nick.

"They don't strike me as the clumsy type," said Tesla.

"Or they *don't* sit near the door," Nick said.

"Whoever's hiding can just move away from wherever they do sit," Tesla replied.

"Or unless the person hiding ate half a leftover burrito for lunch and feels kinda bloated and gassy and, you know, does something about it," said Silas. Silas had eaten half a leftover burrito for lunch, and had been feeling bloated and gassy, and had been quietly doing something about it, off and on, for the past hour.

"Each of them will think the other one's doing it," Tesla said.

"You know what?" DeMarco said. "You talked me into it." He held out a hand to Tesla. "Give me the gadget glove."

Tesla shook her head.

"No. *I'll* do it."

Nick shook his head.

"It was my dumb idea. I'll do it."

Silas shook his head.

"I am Laserhand, master of gadget glove technology. I'll do it."

"No. Really. *I'll* do it," said Tesla.

"No. Really. *I'll* do it," said Nick.

"No. Really. *I'll* do it," said DeMarco.

"No. Really. *I'll* do it," said Silas.

"No. *Really*," Tesla said again, even more firmly than before.

Nick jumped in before she could say "I'll do it." "We don't have time for this! We need to pick someone and get on with it!"

"Fine. We'll decide the way we usually do," said Tesla. "By just doing whatever I say."

"Not this time," said DeMarco. "We'll do rock, paper, scissors."

"Does that even work with four people?" Nick asked.

DeMarco shrugged.

"Let's find out."

He curled his right hand into a fist.

Nick and Tesla and Silas did likewise.

"One. Two. *Three*," said Tesla.

Her hand didn't change. Neither did Nick's and Silas's. They'd all played rock.

DeMarco, however, had flattened his hand. He'd played paper.

He'd won.

"Well, there you go," he said, smiling. "It works."

He flipped his hand over and stretched it toward Tesla.

"Two out of three?" Silas said.

"Just give me the glove and get out of here," De-Marco said to Tesla.

Tesla glowered back at him but went ahead and handed him the glove.

"Ahhh," he sighed as he pulled it on again. "I missed you, buddy."

Silas looked wistfully down at the glove. "I want Glovey back," he whined. "My hand feels all naked without it."

"We should be glad we lost," Nick said to his sister. "Wearing that glove does weird things to people."

"No. It. Does. Not," DeMarco said in a robotic voice. "Now. Must. Destroy. Humans."

He lit up the LED finger and pointed it at Silas.

"*P-shew! P-shew!*"

"Just hide and be quiet, would you?" Tesla snapped. "We're leaving."

DeMarco gave her a final *p-shew* and then flipped off the LED and started toward the far end of the table.

"Good luck," Nick told him.

"Oh, don't worry about me and Glovey," DeMarco said. "We're going to be just fine."

Then he ducked under the table and disappeared from sight.

As Nick, Tesla, and Silas walked off down the hall, they saw Ellen Wharton-Wheeler striding toward them.

Nick and Tesla decided simultaneously to give DeMarco a warning.

"Hi, Ms. Wharton-Wheeler!" they sang sweetly—and loudly. Silas joined in at the end. "—Wheeler."

The tall, dour curator shot them a not-so-sweet look in return.

"You're still here? Isn't your uncle done yet?" she said as she swept past them. "Time's running out, you know."

"Yeah," Tesla said under her breath after they passed by. "For *you*."

Ms. Wharton-Wheeler turned sharply and marched into Meeting Room 2.

The kids lingered in the hallway a moment, waiting for a scream or a furious "What are you doing under there!" But they heard nothing. So far, Nick's "brilliant solution" seemed to be working.

"You know what I don't understand?" Silas whispered. He pointed at the doorway Wharton-Wheeler had just gone through. "I get that she's mad about how things have changed around here. But why would that director lady go along with it? I mean, who'd want to hurt the museum they were in charge of?"

"Ms. Mavis used to work for the Scientastic Explorezone, remember?" Nick said.

Silas nodded slowly, a confused look on his face.

He *didn't* remember.

"She was head of marketing for the museum's biggest rival," Tesla reminded him. "Well, what if she still is? Maybe this is the Scientastic Explorezone's sneakiest marketing campaign ever, if you know what I mean."

The expression on Silas's face didn't change.

He *didn't* know what she meant.

Nick and Tesla shared an exasperated glance.

Then Silas looked suddenly satisfied. "Right!" he said. "It's just like the time the Joker disguised himself as Batman to sneak into Justice League headquarters."

"Yes," Nick said after a moment. "Just like that," Tesla added. "Now let's go before she shows up," she said. "It's gonna look suspicious if we're just hanging around out here."

Tesla meant to lead Nick and Silas back to the Hall of Genius, where DeMarco would go once the secret meeting was over. But she ended up taking a

right when she should have gone left, or taking a left when she should have gone right, or taking a turn when she should have gone straight.

Whichever way it was, the three of them were lost again.

"The next time we try to get anywhere in these hallways, we need to bring a compass and a week's provisions," Tesla said.

"Maybe we should ask the bird for directions," said Nick.

"Bird?"

Nick jerked his thumb at something behind them.

Coolicious McBrainy was stepping out of one of the storerooms about forty feet away.

"Coolicious!" Silas called out. "Hey, man, how do we get back to the lobby?"

The owl shrugged.

Yet again, Coolicious seemed different to Tesla. And not just because his glove was gone and he wasn't dancing.

His owl costume was baggy, bunching up at the ankles, as if it was too big . . . or as if the man inside it had shrunk.

"Well, do you have any idea where we are?" Silas asked.

Coolicious shrugged again and then turned and hurried off with a dull rustling of loose felt and polyester.

"Some mascot. He sees kids and runs away," Nick grumbled. "I guess we'll have to figure this out for ourselves." He turned and read the sign on the nearest door. "Storage 32? Wow. This is the first time we've made it into the thirties. I think we should try a different direction. Maybe take the next right?"

"Your guess is as good as mine," Tesla said.

So they took the next right and found themselves facing yet another long, drab hallway that was identical to the one they'd just left. Almost.

"Now we're getting somewhere!" Tesla said. "Look!"

A small square of color about the size of a credit card was lying on the floor nearby. Nick picked it up.

It was a Migraine Monkey Missile Test refrigerator magnet. Nick had left it there hours before, the second (or was it third?) time they'd gotten lost in the museum's endless halls. On it was a picture of the band. Mojo Jones was in the middle, dressed exactly as he was that day at the Learnasium: jeans, T-shirt, lumberjack shirt. To one side of him was a toweringly tall man wearing a black suit, sunglasses, and a porkpie hat. On his other side was a petite woman with a shaved head, tattered clothes, and tattoos over every visible inch of skin, wearing combat boots that looked six sizes too big for her tiny feet.

"Is that what a ska-punk-emo-metal band's supposed to look like?" Nick asked.

"You forgot the funk," said Silas.

"And the retro grunge twist," said Tesla.

"Whatever," Nick said. He stuffed the magnet into his pocket. "I think I know where we are now. If I'm remembering right, there should be a pair of Migraine Monkey Missile Test underwear around the next corner."

There wasn't. But there was something else lying abandoned on the floor.

"Glovey!" Silas cried.

He ran to the glove, scooped it up, and cradled it

in his arms like an infant.

"The gadget glove?" Nick said. "What's it doing here? And where's DeMarco?"

Tesla didn't say anything. She just walked up to Silas and took the glove from his hand, a grim look on her face.

She pushed the Play button on the sound chip, and they heard a voice.

It was DeMarco's.

"Guys, if you find this . . . it's me," he said.

DeMarco was speaking in a breathy staticky whisper, and a steady thud of quick footsteps could be heard, too. It sounded as if was holding the recording chip close to his mouth while walking fast.

"Things didn't exactly go according to plan," he went on.

A new noise rose in the background—a quick *sh-sh-sh* swishing.

"Whatever's going on here, it's way weirder than we thought," DeMarco said, "and now I think I'm—hey!"

There was a burst of loud, distorted sound.

Then silence.

"Ready?" said Uncle Newt.

"Ready," said Hiroko.

They each reached out a hand toward the keyboard and together they hit Enter.

Once again, the Hall of Genius came to life.

Lights brightened, machines hummed.

No prominent scientists or inventors went cuckoo or flew apart.

So far, so good.

Next Uncle Newt walked over to the Nikola Tesla display and pushed the big red button there.

"Hello," robo-Tesla said. "Would

you like me to show you how an induction motor works?"

"Yes," answered Uncle Newt.

"Excellent. It is really quite interesting. The key is creating a rotating magnetic field."

And on Nikola Tesla went, talking, demonstrating his motor, neither going cuckoo nor flying apart. Uncle Newt let him run through his whole spiel before turning to Hiroko with a smile.

"Looks like we made it," he said.

Hiroko nodded. She looked relieved. And tired.

"With all of an hour to go before the rededication ceremony," she said. "I just wish we knew what went wrong before."

Uncle Newt shrugged.

"A power surge, a short, gremlins . . . who knows? Whatever it was, obviously it was a fluke. The important thing is that the Hall of Genius is ready, and we can finally relax."

Just then Nick, Tesla, and Silas burst through the door near the Einstein display.

"DeMarco's been kidnapped!" Tesla cried.

"What?" Uncle Newt and Hiroko said in unison as the kids ran toward them.

"Well, maybe captured would be more accurate," said Nick.

"Or caught," Tesla added.

"Kidnapped, captured, whatever," Silas snapped. "The point is they got him!"

"Who got him? What is going on?" Uncle Newt asked.

"Nick, you tell him," Tesla said. "You're better at synopsizing than me."

Nick nodded, sucked in a long, deep breath, and then began to explain:

"Tesla thought the Hall of Genius had been sabotaged so we took a look at Ms. Wharton-Wheeler's computer because she obviously doesn't like the animatronics in here and we saw that she'd exchanged e-mails with Katherine Mavis with the subject heading 'Destroying the Museum from Within' so we figured the two of them were in on it together and then we found out they were having a meeting so we figured out a way to record part of it to get proof and DeMarco was hiding in the room where they were going to be talking and—"

Nick doubled over, gasping for breath.

"He was wearing this when we last saw him,"

Tesla continued for her brother, holding up the gadget glove. "We found it lying in the hall. It's got one of Uncle Newt's sound chips built into it. This is what it recorded."

Tesla turned on the chip.

"Guys, if you find this . . . it's me," they heard DeMarco say. "Things didn't exactly go according to plan. Whatever's going on here, it's way weirder than we thought, and now I think I'm—hey!"

"What's that noise in the background?" Uncle Newt asked. "The shushing?"

"We don't know," said Nick.

"It does sound weirdly familiar," said Tesla.

"Forget the shushing!" Silas blurted out. "What's that noise at the end? It sounds like someone's beating DeMarco with a bag of frying pans!"

"I think it's just distortion, Silas," Hiroko said gently. "DeMarco probably put his hand over the sound chip when he was taking off the glove. That was clever of him to drop it for you to find."

"So you believe us?" Nick asked.

"Well, whether there was sabotage or not, something's definitely happened to DeMarco," Hiroko said. She turned to Uncle Newt, her expression grave. "We need to do something."

Uncle Newt nodded.

"There's only one thing to do," he said. "We need to take this to the professionals."

If Tesla had known *which* professional Uncle Newt would end up taking it to, she would have talked him out of it.

"Let me get this straight," Berg said. "You want me to listen to a talking glove?"

The squat, strapping guard had been sitting at his boss's desk in the security office when the group had come in.

"Chief Ruffin's got important business to attend to elsewhere right now," he'd told them. "So he left me in charge."

When they'd told him that DeMarco had disappeared, leaving behind what sounded like a recording of his kidnapping via a gadget-covered glove, Berg had squinted at them like they were crazy.

"Just listen, would you?" Hiroko snapped. "Play DeMarco's message, Tesla."

Tesla turned on the sound chip.

Yet even as he listened, Berg's skeptical squint didn't disappear.

"What does he mean about things not going according to plan and being weirder than you thought?" Berg asked when DeMarco's message came to an abrupt end. He was speaking to Uncle Newt and Hiroko, expecting the adults to explain.

"The kids had some suspicions about the malfunction in the Hall of Genius," Uncle Newt said. "But that's not what matters right now. We have to find—"

"It *does* matter!" Tesla interrupted. "If we're right, then we know who's got DeMarco!" She turned to Berg and tried to muster all the conviction she could. "We think the museum's being sabotaged . . ." But then her confidence—and her voice—cracked. "By Ms. Mavis and Ms. Wharton-Wheeler."

Berg gave her the look of disgust she was dreading.

"Is this a prank?" he asked.

"No!" said Tesla.

"Are you punking me?"

"No!" said Nick.

"Is this a loyalty test? Something the chief put you up to?"

"No!" said Silas and Hiroko and Uncle Newt.

"Well, then, you're all nuts," said Berg.

"Look, that recording isn't fake," Nick told him. "You can hear it. Somebody grabbed our friend."

"And you're supposed to do something about it!" Silas threw in. "Do your job, dude!"

For a second, it looked as if Berg's job, as he saw it, might be picking up Silas and hurling him out of the room like a shot put. But then the fury drained from his face, leaving behind only the contempt from before.

Berg picked up a phone from the desk and punched in three numbers.

"When the police get here, you can straighten all this out with them," he said. "And if they decide to haul you in for filing a false report, that won't be my fault. Yes, hello. This is security officer Donald F. Berg over at the X-Treme Learnasium. We've got a possible child abduction situation here. Who's reporting it? Some kids. Friends of the alleged victim. No. No witnesses. All right. Thanks."

Berg hung up.

"They're going to send a car over when they can."

"When will that be?" Uncle Newt asked.

Berg glared at him.

"When. They. Can."

"So what are we gonna do in the meantime?" said Tesla.

"What do you mean, what are we gonna do?" said Berg. "You're going to wait, that's what."

"Just wait?" said Hiroko. "While a boy is missing somewhere in your museum?"

"Exactly," Berg said. "Do you see that?"

He reached out and tapped one of the video monitors near his boss's desk. It showed the museum's main atrium, which was no longer dark and deserted. Overhead lights had been turned on, and men and women in white shirts and black pants were taking positions here and there holding big silver trays.

"Any minute now, some very important people are going to walk in there for a very important event," he said. "I can't waste my time looking for a very *un*important kid who's decided to play hide-and-seek."

"Unimportant? *Unimportant?*" Uncle Newt spat,

looking madder than his niece and nephew had ever seen him. "Why, you obstinate, obtuse, officious martinet!"

Berg leaned forward and planted his fists on the desk.

"You're lucky I don't know what any of those things are," he growled.

Hiroko stepped between Berg and Uncle Newt and turned to face Nick and Tesla.

"You know, the police are only going to need one of us here with Mr. Berg to make the report," she said. "Why don't you give me the sound chip so I can play it when the officers get here? Then the rest of you can go try to . . . relax."

She gave the kids a wink.

"Thanks, Hiroko," said Nick.

"Yeah. Good thinking," said Tesla.

"What? I can't relax at a time like this!" said Silas.

"Tell me about it!" said Uncle Newt. "I'm all worked up!"

"But what can you really do until the police arrive?" Hiroko said, winking again—first at Silas, then at Uncle Newt.

"Are you okay?" Silas asked her.

"Something in your eye?" asked Uncle Newt.

Tesla couldn't take it anymore. She shoved the gadget glove into Hiroko's hands and then grabbed Uncle Newt and began tugging him toward the door.

"Oh, just come on!"

Nick took hold of Silas and dragged him out, too.

"Hey!" Berg said, starting to stand up. "Wait!"

Hiroko stepped in front of him again, blocking his view of the doorway.

"Tell me, Officer," she said, gazing at him admiringly. "Do you work out?"

"Oh. Yeah. I do, actually," Berg said, instantly forgetting about Uncle Newt and the kids. He lifted an arm and flexed a biceps the size of a pot roast. "Does it show?"

"I get it!" Uncle Newt said as he, Tesla, Nick, and Silas walked off up the hall. "Go relax, wink-wink. But we're *not* going to relax, are we?"

"We're going to look for DeMarco!" said Silas, finally getting it, too.

Nick and Tesla shared a long-suffering look.

"Yes. That's right," Tesla said. "Berg didn't believe us, and there's no guarantee the police will either. So we need to start searching on our own."

"Where, though?" Nick asked. "There are so many storage rooms in this place, we could look for a year and never find DeMarco. Assuming he's still in the building at all."

"Thanks for pointing out why we're doomed to fail, Little Mr. Sunshine," Tesla said.

"That's what I'm here for," Nick said.

"Maybe we should check Ms. Mavis's office," Silas suggested. "Or the exhibit the curator lady's been working on."

Tesla thought it over for a moment without slowing her pace.

"No, I don't think so," she finally said. "Ms. Mavis couldn't have gotten DeMarco into her office without someone noticing, and any second now Ms. Wharton-Wheeler's space exhibit is going to be opened for the gala."

"Where *do* we start, then?" Silas asked.

"I have no idea," said Tesla.

Uncle Newt tapped her on the shoulder.

"Uh, then where are you leading us?"

Tesla finally noticed that she'd moved out in front of the others, striding forward purposefully without knowing where she was going.

She stopped so suddenly that Silas, Nick, and Uncle Newt almost plowed right over her.

"Uncle Newt," she said, "what do we do?"

Uncle Newt blinked at her, seemingly surprised to find his niece turning to him for advice just because she was eleven and he was forty.

"Well, I'm afraid the first thing we need to do," he said, "is call DeMarco's parents and let them know he's missing."

Nick and Tesla grimaced.

DeMarco's mom and dad already distrusted the twins. Now they were going to *hate* them.

Uncle Newt slipped a hand into one of the pockets of his white lab coat, pulled out his wallet, and without looking at it put it to his ear.

"That's weird," he said. "I can't get a signal."

"Um, there's a reason for that," Nick said, pointing at the wallet.

"Oh. Right."

Uncle Newt stuffed the wallet back into his

pocket and pulled out a phone.

"That's weird," he said a moment later. "I'm still not getting a signal."

He checked to make sure he was trying to call on a phone and not a candy bar or a pocket calculator. But it was a phone, and there was no signal.

"Oh, well. Guess I'll have to try again later."

Uncle Newt put his phone away and then slapped his hands together and gave them a rub.

"All righty. Now we need to appraise our data."

"Do what now?" Silas said.

"Think about what we know," Nick explained.

"And what we *don't* know," Uncle Newt said. "The X factors. The unknown quantities."

"Okay. We know that someone grabbed DeMarco. We don't know who," Silas said. "Now, where do we go and what do we do?"

Uncle Newt shook his head. "We *think* someone grabbed DeMarco. But maybe he was running and dropped the glove. Maybe he got away from whoever was chasing him and got lost. Maybe he was apprehended by one of the security guards, and they didn't phone it in to Borg."

"Berg," Tesla corrected him.

"And you're forgetting something else we don't know," Uncle Newt continued.

"Where they took him?" Silas guessed.

"Yes, there's that, of course. But I was thinking of the *sh-sh-sh*."

"The what-what-what?" said Silas.

Sh-sh-sh-sh-sh. It was a swishing sound, just like the one they'd heard on DeMarco's recording.

"Yes! That's it! Very good!" Uncle Newt said, turning back to Tesla.

"I'm not doing it," she said.

Uncle Newt looked at Nick.

"Me, neither."

The swishing was growing louder.

Shuffling up the hall behind the group was Coolicious McBrainy. The *sh-sh-sh* was the sound of the polyester "feathers" on his legs rustling as he walked.

"So the owl grabbed DeMarco?" Silas cracked his knuckles. "Let's get him."

"Wait," said Tesla.

She noticed that Coolicious was wearing his glove again. And now his costume didn't seem baggy like it had the last time she'd seen him.

So, Tesla decided, there was another X factor to

consider: what was up with this big bird? Not only did his outfit keep changing, but this time he was ranting loudly as he marched up the hallway.

"Unacceptable! Unforgivable! Intolerable!"

And then he did something *really* surprising.

He reached up both wings, ripped off his head, and threw it on the floor.

"Unscrupulous! Unethical! Insulting!" spat his new head—the human one that had been inside the owl head all along.

Coolicious McBrainy, it turned out, was a fifty-ish man with short-cropped red hair and a mustache as thick and bristly as a scrub brush. His eyes were wild, his face beaded with perspiration.

He kept stripping off the rest of his suit, leaving each piece on the floor as he continued up the hallway.

"Sorry to disillusion you, kids," he said as he got closer. "But Coolicious McBrainy is not really a magical intellectual hipster-teen owl."

"We guessed that," Nick muttered.

Coolicious—or whatever his real name was—didn't hear him.

"I'm just a man," he raved. "A disrespected, disposable man. And I will not stand for this kind of treatment!"

The upper half of his suit was completely peeled off at this point, revealing a tight sweat-dampened T-shirt beneath. He stopped walking, ripped off his oversized talon-shaped boots, and tossed them over his shoulder.

"Uh, excuse me," Tesla said. "But have you seen our friend DeMarco? Twelve years old? Kinda short?"

"No. Sorry," the man said.

Now he was peeling the Coolicious costume off his legs. Underneath he was wearing yellow short-shorts that barely reached the tops of his surprisingly muscular thighs.

"May I ask why you're undressing in a hallway?" Uncle Newt asked.

"Because I'm quitting, that's why!" the man said with a snarl. "I'm a professional. An artist! I've been a tap-dancing Pikachu. A break-dancing Burger King. I did an ice-skating Snoopy that brought thousands to tears! And these ingrates don't even have the common courtesy to tell me that I'll be out there vamping with a bunch of rank amateurs!"

"What are you talking about?" Silas said.

The man finished pulling off the rest of his costume, wadded it up into a big ball, and threw it against the wall.

"Just go look and you'll see," he said, flapping a hand at the pair of double doors at the far end of the hallway. "They took my backup suits and gave them to a bunch of imposters. *I* was supposed to be the X-Treme Learnasium's mascot. *I* was supposed to be Coolicious McBrainy, the raddest screech owl to ever give a hoot about science and technology! And now I find out I'm just another piece of meat in a feather suit? I won't stand for it!"

And with that the man stomped off, his sweat-soaked socks leaving a trail of moist footprints as he went.

"We're just gonna let him go?" Silas said.

"Weren't you listening?" said Tesla. "Our pool of suspects just got a lot bigger."

She headed toward the double doors at the end of the hall. Nick, Uncle Newt, and Silas followed after her.

Soon they heard music. Then laughter. Then voices. Lots of them.

It was obvious what was going on.

The X-Treme Learnasium's grand rededication gala had begun.

When the four of them reached the doors, they opened them a crack and peeked through. The cavernous atrium lobby was well lit. Dozens of people in tuxedoes and shimmery dresses were scattered all around, happily chattering among the display cases and demonstration booths and giant slimy-looking organs. Two women—one dressed as an astronaut, the other as an explorer—were busily handing out drinks from behind a makeshift bar in front of the gift shop, while several waiters dressed in suits with black bow ties moved smoothly through the crowd carrying platters of hors d'oeuvres.

The animatronic Tyrannosaurus and Triceratops at the center of the huge room suddenly threw back their heads and roared, and the partygoers gasped . . . and then applauded.

"Oooh," Silas moaned as a waiter passed nearby. "Pigs in blankets!"

"I think those are shrimp puffs," said Nick.

"Whatever. I'm starving."

Silas started to push through the doors. But Tesla pulled him back.

"Come on!" he protested. "Do you know how long it's been since lunch?"

"About six hours," Tesla said without looking at him. She was scanning the room for owls. "But we can't just barge in and start chomping on shrimp puffs. We've got to lie low till we know who has De-Marco."

"All right," Silas whined. "I just wish I could lie low with something in my stomach."

Nick elbowed his sister in the side.

"Check it out, Tez. They've opened the other new wings."

Tesla swung her gaze up to Ms. Wharton-Wheeler's space exhibit on the second-floor landing. The big white partitions had been removed, revealing an entrance that was built to look like a space station airlock. Next to it, written in big blocky silver letters, were the words WHATEVER HAPPENED TO THE FINAL FRONTIER?

Back on the first floor, the other wing that had been closed off was on the other side of the dinosaurs, and Tesla had to lean to the side to get a look at the entrance. She could see a round entryway ringed with yellow neon. Extending in an arc over top was the name of the exhibit:

something NEW under the sun

Tesla assumed the Hall of Genius had been opened, too, though it wasn't visible from where they were standing. Which meant that if the saboteurs had been trying to stop the X-Treme Learnasium's public debut, they'd failed.

But maybe that wasn't what they were after. There had to be another goal, a bigger plan. Tesla was sure of that now. But what was it?

"If it's those other owls you're looking for, there they are," said Uncle Newt. "One by the T-Rex's tail, one by the giant liver, and one over there by the bar."

"Wow. Good eye, Uncle Newt," said Tesla. "I can still barely see 'em."

Uncle Newt gave her a humble shrug.

"I was into bird watching when I was a kid."

"So we know one of them was near DeMarco when he was captured," Nick said. "But how do we figure out which?"

"I'm not sure. We need to get close, see what they're up to, but we've gotta be subtle about it," said Tesla. "We don't want the bad guys to panic and make a break for it."

"What do you think, Uncle Newt?" Nick asked. "What should we—hey. Where'd he go?"

"He was here just a second ago," Tesla said.

They turned around to find their uncle walking toward them carrying a giant owl head.

"It would seem that whoever is behind this has figured out a pretty good disguise," Uncle Newt said. He put the owl head over his own.

"Why can't we use it, too?"

"Oh, my," Uncle Newt said when he was zipped into the Coolicious suit.

"What's wrong?" asked Nick.

"I can see why that actor was wearing such skimpy clothes. It is *hot* in here."

Within seconds, Uncle Newt could feel his shirt growing soggy with sweat.

"And damp," he added.

He inhaled deeply to make sure he'd be able to breathe in the tight-fitting outfit.

"And stinky. Now I know why there were so many backup costumes. Wearing this thing is like being mummified in dirty sweat socks. Oh, well. Wish me luck!"

"Good luck," Nick, Tesla, and Silas said.

Uncle Newt saluted them with a wing and then turned and pushed through the double doors into the atrium.

It took him a moment to get his bearings. The owl head had two eyeholes the size of coasters, but they were covered with a fine metal mesh to hide the person wearing the suit. The mesh blurred everything Uncle Newt saw, turning the world into a collection of indistinct blobs.

Finding the other Cooliciouses wasn't going to be easy.

There was only one thing to do.

Mingle.

So this is what being responsible gets you, Uncle Newt thought as he shuffled toward the crowd. *You agree to look after your niece and nephew for a few weeks and you end up hunting kidnappers in a smelly owl suit.*

It occurred to him that it was a good thing he didn't have children of his own. If this was what parenting was like, he probably wouldn't survive.

But there was no turning back now. He'd been neglecting the kids all day, and now there was a price to pay. It was up to him to make sure Mario was safe.

Or was it DeMarcus? Delmonte?

Great. A boy's life was in his hands, and he couldn't even remember the kid's name.

Uncle Newt loved Nick and Tesla, but for the first time he found himself wishing they'd gone to stay with their Aunt Hypatia.

"*Another* owl?" he heard someone chuckle.

He turned toward the voice and saw a blob that had the general shape of a human male.

"Sure. We're a flock," Uncle Newt said. "Could you steer me toward the nearest one? I'm a little lost."

The blob pointed. Uncle Newt couldn't see what exactly he was pointing at, but at least he could tell the direction.

"Well, must fly," Uncle Newt said. "Birds of a feather and all that."

He moved off as quickly as he dared.

Uncle Newt was in among the gala guests now. Two hundred of San Francisco's most prestigious philanthropists, business leaders, journalists, and "notables," as Katherine Mavis had put it when she described the guest list to him. She was going to give a speech, let the mayor or the governor or the pope or somebody cut a symbolic ribbon (Uncle Newt hadn't really been paying attention), and then take the crowd on a tour. First they'd see "the showstopper" (whatever that was), then the Hall of Genius, then Ms. Wharton-Wheeler's exhibit upstairs. Uncle Newt had assumed he'd be home tinkering in his basement lab when all the hoopla happened, not stumbling through the middle of it, half blind.

Then he bumped into something just soft enough—barely—to be a person. A shrill voice screeched, "Ahhh! Red wine! On my Givenchy!"

Uncle Newt wasn't sure what a "givenchy" was, but he assumed it was either an expensive dress or a part of the human anatomy with which he was unfamiliar.

He reached out and found himself patting a bony shoulder.

"Bill it to the museum," he said.

Once again, he beat a hasty retreat. Not too hasty, though. There were only so many notables he could drench in red wine before the wrong owl noticed.

"We're ska-funk-punk-emo-metal with a retro grunge twist," he heard a familiar voice say. "And I—

oh! Is everything all right?"

Uncle Newt leaned in close to see who was talking to him. So close, in fact, that he ended up bonking Mojo Jones on the head with his beak.

"Hey! Ow!"

"Sorry! Everything's fine! Hoo-hoo! Science is cool!"

Uncle Newt moved on.

"Um, well, as I was saying, I rap," he heard Mojo say after a long silence. Uncle Newt thought he sounded strangely shaken, though perhaps that was natural for someone who'd just been pecked by a giant owl.

Canned jazz music had been playing in the background as Uncle Newt wandered through the crowd, but now it faded out and an amplified voice echoed through the atrium.

"Ladies and gentlemen, welcome to the new and improved Northern California Museum of Science, Industry, and Technology. The X-Treme Learnasium!"

It was Katherine Mavis. The crowd responded with polite applause.

"Tonight you, our special friends, have the honor

of being the first to tour the X-Treme Learnasium," she went on. "I think you're going to find what you see inspiring, delightful, and, in at least one case, very, very surprising."

A wave of excited murmurs spread through the room, though whoever the woman was who was standing next to Uncle Newt wasn't talking about the Learnasium. She was saying, "Put down your phone and have a meatball, Frank."

"Have a meatball, she says. Have a meatball!" this Frank grumbled back. "With our stocks dropping like lead balloons and our broker backpacking over the Andes. And to top it all off, I can't even get a signal on a $5,000 cell phone! Where are we, anyway? The moon?"

"So there's nothing you can do," the woman replied. "Have a meatball."

"Why are you pushing meatballs on me all of a sudden? What's in the sauce? Arsenic?"

The woman sighed loudly.

Uncle Newt couldn't see the squabbling couple. He couldn't see any of the owls. He couldn't see anything. He was no closer to finding Nick and Tesla's friend than he had been when he put on the suit.

Time for a game changer, he decided.

"Excuse me," Uncle Newt said, turning toward (he hoped) Frank and his lady friend. "Did they happen to give you a fork for the meatballs?"

"What? No," the woman said, sounding surprised. "They're on toothpicks."

"Oh."

"But they gave me a fork for the oysters," the woman said.

"Ah! Could I borrow it for a second?"

"Uh, sure."

Uncle Newt stretched out a hand—or a wing—and after a moment he felt the woman drop the fork into it.

Then he tightened his grip on the utensil and plunged it into his right eye. Coolicious McBrainy's right eye, that is.

He could hear the woman gasp as he stabbed at the eye over and over, ripping a hole in the wire mesh. When the hole was big enough, Uncle Newt turned back to the woman. He could see her now. She had short gray hair and jewels around her neck and a shocked look on her pale face. Next to her was, he assumed, Frank—a gaunt, glowering old man with a cell phone in one hand and the other clenched into a fist.

Uncle Newt quickly gave the woman back her fork.

"Enjoy the oysters."

He moved away, scanning the room as he went. He had only a little porthole about the size of a quarter to see through, but it was an improvement.

There was Katherine Mavis standing behind a podium, saying more about the exciting new this and the awesome new that at the Learnasium.

There was Ms. Wharton-Wheeler standing behind her, looking neither excited nor awed.

There were two Coolicious McBrainys, one tall, one small, lingering at the edge of the crowd, not far from the guards—*guards?*—stationed in front of the *Something NEW under the Sun* exhibit.

And there was the third Coolicious on the opposite side of the atrium, walking toward the Hall of Genius.

And stepping over the velvet rope stretched across the entrance.

And slinking off into the hall.

"Gotcha," Uncle Newt said to himself.

He'd found the bad egg.

He moved quickly(ish) toward the Hall of Genius, trying—and quite often failing—not to jostle any bigwigs or splash them with their cocktails. He was now sweating so profusely he could feel half an inch of pooled perspiration squishing beneath his feet with every step. His eyes were stinging, his head was beginning to swim. But on he hurried.

Just hold on, what's-your-name! Uncle Newt thought. *I'm coming for you!*

At last he cleared the crowd and scurried past the museum's giant pancreas, then the giant gall bladder, then the giant brain. When he reached the velvet rope blocking off the Hall of Genius, he jumped into the air, flapping his wings to give himself every bit of lift possible.

He soared over the rope, hit the ground running, and dashed into the hall.

Inisde, he found the other Coolicious, bent over the control panel hidden in Sir Alexander Fleming's lab. He was trying to type something into the keypad but seemed to be having a hard time.

"Stupid wings," the owl groused.

"Hold it right there!" Uncle Newt shouted.

The owl looked up in surprise, then spun on his heel and tore off toward Einstein's blackboard.

So the evil owl knew about the control panel *and* the secret back exit. If he made it out through the door, he would disappear in the museum's endless corridors.

Uncle Newt was already panting and nearly blinded by sweat, but he swerved toward the blackboard and pushed himself to run even harder. And then he quickly tripped over Sir Isaac Newton's foot.

"Nooooooo!" he cried as he crashed to the floor.

For a moment, Uncle Newt lay there stunned, cursing gravity. Then he pushed himself to his knees, expecting to see the rear exit door open and the other owl long gone.

Instead he saw this: the owl running past him with Silas on his heels while Nick and Tesla stood in the doorway by Einstein's blackboard, their eyes open wide.

Of course, Uncle Newt realized. The kids had been watching as he'd stumbled through the reception. When they saw he was heading for the Hall of Genius—and why he was heading there—they'd taken the back way to cut off any escape. But could they

really keep the owl-man from getting away?

Uncle Newt quickly got his answer: Silas threw himself on the bird's back in a flying tackle, and the two of them hit the ground in a heap.

"Oof!" said the owl.

"Got ya!" said Silas.

The owl tried to get up, but Silas stayed on his back, pinning him down.

"I sure hope that's you in there, Uncle Newt," Nick said, walking up cautiously to his uncle. "Otherwise, Silas owes you a big apology, and I'm talking to the bad guy."

"It's me, Nick. Would you help me get this head off? I'm about to suffocate in here."

Nick undid the Velcro holding the head in place, then pulled it off.

"Air!" Uncle Newt rasped. He sucked in a deep breath. "Oh, sweet, unsweaty, 20.95 percent oxygen air, how I love you!"

Nick gave the inside of the head a sniff, then scowled and went pale.

"All right. Let's see who's behind all this," Tesla said.

She walked to the other owl, bent down beside

him, and ripped off his head.

"Oh," she said, stepping back from the stranger beneath the mask. "Who the heck are you?"

Staring back up at Tesla was a red-faced man with cracked, crooked glasses and a dark goatee.

"Mark!" Uncle Newt said. "I'm disappointed in you! Don't think I won't tell the Multinational Alliance of Developmental Scientists about this!"

"Is that Mark Carstairs?" asked Nick. "The designer who got fired when the Hall of Genius wouldn't work?"

"It is, indeed."

The man tried to say something, but all that came out was a wheeze. His face was turning a dark purple.

"Maybe you ought to let the guy breathe, Silas," Tesla suggested.

"Right." Silas slid off the man's back but remained hovering over him, ready to slam on him again at a moment's notice. "We don't want him to smother before he tells us where DeMarco is."

"Exactly," Tesla said. She looked at Carstairs with disgust. "So, you came back to get revenge on the museum."

Uncle Newt expected him to sneer, "Yes, and I would've gotten away with it if not for you meddling kids and your giant owl."

Instead, once the man took in a few breaths and his face didn't look so much like a big red grape, he said this:

"You've got it all wrong. I know this is going to sound crazy, but I think there's a conspiracy to destroy the museum. I'm here to stop it!"

13

"He's lying," Silas said. "Want me to sit on him?"

"No! Please!" Carstairs begged. He was still stretched out flat on the floor, helplessly spread-eagled on his stomach as Silas swiveled around and got set to plop back down on him like a beanbag chair.

"Wait," Tesla said.

Silas froze midsquat.

"You're here to save the museum?" she said to Carstairs. "By sneaking around in a mascot costume?"

"Yes!" Carstairs squeaked, eyeing Silas's hovering haunches with dread. "Just let me explain!"

Tesla and Nick and Uncle Newt looked at one another.

"We should at least hear him out," Uncle Newt said.

Nick nodded his agreement.

"Okay, Silas," Tesla said. "Let him speak."

Silas frowned, obviously unconvinced their prisoner would tell the truth without a thorough squashing first. But he turned and sat on the floor again all the same.

Carstairs sighed with relief and then began talking.

"While I was building all this"—he said, flapping a feathered hand at the animatronic figures around them—"I started noticing minor adjustments to the control settings. Little changes I couldn't account for. I figured it was a glitch in the software, but I could never pin it down. Eventually, I started to suspect someone was experimenting with the control dashboard. Someone who was getting access to it through the museum's network."

"Meaning, someone who works for the museum," Tesla said.

"Or a hacker. But why would someone like that care about the Hall of Genius?" said Carstairs. "The more I tried to figure out what was going on, the more problems I had with the animatronics. It finally got so bad that the whole Hall of Genius locked up. I tried to tell Katherine Mavis that someone was sabotaging me, but she thought I was just making excuses. All she cared about was a guarantee that everything would be ready for tonight. And when I couldn't give her one, she replaced me."

Carstairs turned his gaze on Uncle Newt.

"And let me guess," he said. "You've been having trouble, too."

"It was smooth as can be until today, actually," Uncle Newt said. "Then suddenly, just like that— "

Uncle Newt tried to snap, but between the owl costume and his fingers being slick with sweat, he couldn't manage it. He gave up after three tries.

"Anyway," Uncle Newt said, "everything went cuckoo. It seems fine now, but we never did figure out what went wrong."

"See!" Carstairs cried. "They're still doing it! Messing with the controls! I wanted to come back and prove it, but there was no way Ms. Mavis was going to let me regain access to the Hall of Genius. So . . . well . . . I found this extra costume, and I improvised."

Nick looked over at his sister and uncle.

He was about to say "What do you think?" but before he could open his mouth, Silas rose to a crouch.

"I still don't believe him," he said. "It's squishin' time!"

He started to lower himself onto a whimpering Carstairs.

"Silas! Stop it!" Tesla commanded in the tone most people reserve for "No! Bad dog!"

Sulky and sour faced, Silas straightened and crossed his arms across his broad chest.

"Why are you so obsessed with sitting on people?" Nick asked.

"I'm good at it," Silas said with a pout.

"Kids," said Uncle Newt, "I *do* believe Mark."

"Yeah . . . I think I do, too," Nick said slowly.

Tesla nodded. "If he was the one who messed up the controls earlier today," she said, "then why would he need to be here now? He could just keep hacking in from wherever. So, yes—I think he's telling the truth."

Carstairs heaved a sigh of relief.

"Can I stand up now?" he asked.

"Yes," Tesla said.

Silas kept sulking but didn't make any threatening moves.

"Well, this has been fascinating," Uncle Newt said, "but it hasn't gotten us any closer to finding DeMarco."

He walked to Sir Alexander Fleming's laboratory and picked up the phone mounted by the control panel.

"What are you doing?" Carstairs asked.

Uncle Newt punched in three numbers and then put the phone to his ear.

"We have a young friend who's gone missing," he said to Carstairs. "We thought you could tell us where he is. But now that we know you can't . . ."

Carstairs looked like he wanted to lie back down on the floor and let Silas flatten him.

"You're calling the police?"

"Re-calling them, actually. They were supposed to be here by now. I'm sorry, Mark. I know you could get in trouble for trespassing and impersonating an owl and all. But the clock is ticking and—yes, hello?" Uncle Newt held up a finger and focused his attention on the phone. "I'm calling from the X-Treme Learnasium on Kearny Street. Or maybe it's on Stockton. Or Chestnut? I'm one of those people who navigates by landmarks, not street names. Sometimes I even forget my own address! Anyhoo, I'm in that big glass building? Looks kind of like the Great Pyramid of Giza, but more see-through? Used to be called the Northern California Museum of Science, Industry, and—yes! That's it! Powell Street! Well, we have a bit of a situation here and— oh, really? Really? *Really?* Okay, then. Thank you."

Uncle Newt hung up the phone with a puzzled, perturbed look on his face.

"What did they say?" Nick asked.

"That they knew about the earlier call. That a squad car would be here any second."

"So what's the problem?" said Tesla.

"I could've sworn I heard Katherine Mavis speaking in the background."

Everyone was silent for a moment. So silent that they could hear Katherine Mavis's voice echoing in from the atrium.

". . . anxious to begin our tour," she was saying. "But before we show you the wonders of the X-Treme Learnasium, there are a few people I should thank . . ."

"Are you sure you heard it coming over the phone?" Tesla asked.

Uncle Newt nodded.

"Could it have been some kind of interference from the P.A. system?" asked Nick.

Uncle Newt shook his head.

"If—if someone could access the museum's network and sabotage the Hall of Genius," Tesla asked, "could they reroute 911 calls to a personal cell phone?"

Uncle Newt nodded slowly.

"So you think you were talking to the bad guy just now?" Nick asked.

To Nick's immense disappointment, his uncle nodded again.

"Was it a man or a woman?" Tesla asked.

This time, Uncle Newt shrugged.

"You can't tell when you're talking to a man or a woman?" Silas asked, incredulous.

Uncle Newt shrugged again. "Whoever they

were, they were trying to disguise their voice. It was muffled, squeaky. It could have been a woman with a low voice or a man with a high voice."

"Do you think Berg was talking to the same person when *he* called 911?" Tesla asked.

"The fact that the cops haven't shown up answers that question," Nick said miserably. He perked up for a moment, struck by a thought, but then drooped again, looking more miserable than ever. "Unless Berg didn't call 911 at all. For all we know, he's the mastermind behind whatever's going on."

Tesla looked skeptical that Berg could be the mastermind behind anything.

"Or it could be his boss, Ruffin," she said. "He'd have access to all the museum's security codes and communications systems and stuff."

"Oh, man. What if *all* the guards are in on it?" Silas said. "That's a lot of people to sit on . . ."

"Well, there is a simple way to resolve all this," Carstairs announced. His wings went limp, and something began slithering around beneath his owl chest.

Carstairs grimaced, contorted his shoulders,

and then said, "There. Got it."

Out of the neck hole of his suit popped a hand holding a cell phone.

"Eww," he said. "It's kinda slimy."

He managed to push some buttons on it anyway.

Then he pushed the buttons again.

"That's weird," he said. "I was going to call the police myself, but I can't get a signal."

"I couldn't get one either," said Uncle Newt. "And I heard someone at the party saying the same thing."

"Jammers?" said Carstairs.

"It's possible," said Uncle Newt.

Both men fell silent, looking uneasy yet impressed.

"So the police aren't coming and we can't call them," Nick said. "DeMarco is still missing, and we have no idea who the bad guys are or what they're up to."

"Yeah," Uncle Newt murmured. "That sums it up pretty well, Nick. You *are* good at synopsizing."

"So what are we gonna do?" Silas asked.

When no one answered him, he instinctively

turned to Tesla. She always knew what to do. Or she acted like she did, anyway.

But not this time.

Tesla just stared back at Silas, speechless. Then she abruptly turned away, unable to face the dawning disappointment and fear she saw in her friend's eyes.

"It's all my fault," she said softly. "Whatever happens to DeMarco, I caused it."

The boy loved taking stupid risks, Tesla told herself. But this was one she'd steered him toward. She'd steered all of them toward it. And why? Not just because she was worried about her uncle's reputation or what might happen to the museum. There was something more.

Tesla felt a hand on her shoulder.

Her brother had stepped up beside her.

"Maybe you were right about me this morning, Nick," she said to him. "Maybe I can't fix the big problem—getting our parents back—so I go looking for other problems to fix."

"Tesla—"

"Or maybe I'm just becoming as much of an adrenaline addict as DeMarco—"

"Tesla." Nick interrupted her with that firm voice he hardly ever used. "We'll figure something out," he said to her. "I know we will."

"I—"

"Hey," he continued. "Don't give up now. *They* didn't give up, right?"

They? For a second, Tesla didn't know what "they" Nick was talking about. Then she remembered where she was: the Hall of Genius. And right after that, she remembered who else was in the room.

Marie Curie. She'd been excluded, dismissed, denigrated, but that didn't stop her from becoming one of the most groundbreaking scientists of her time.

Copernicus, Kepler, and Galileo. All accused of heresy, mocked, and even threatened for suggesting the Earth isn't the center of the universe. Despite that, their ideas eventually persevered.

Even her namesake, Nikola Tesla, had been forced to endure his share of hardships.

"Tesla!" Tesla blurted out. "That's the key to everything!"

"Is she talking to herself?" Silas asked.

Nick was too busy smacking himself on the forehead to answer.

"Yes! Of course!" he said as his sister hurried over to the Nikola Tesla display. He darted after her.

Side by side, they stared down at the duct tape covering part of the inventor's biography. Without a word, they began picking at the tape, Tesla working on one end, Nick the other. After a few seconds, they each had enough tape peeled to grab and pull hard.

And this is what they saw:

In 1901, Tesla began building what became known as "The Tesla Tower," a power plant designed to wirelessly transmit electricity. Unfortunately, it was the visionary inventor's greatest failure. The tower never worked and was eventually torn down. But a century later, the solar power pioneers at Solanow have made Tesla's dream of wireless energy transfer a reality—one that you can see for yourself in our exhibit

SOMETHING NEW UNDER THE SUN!

Tesla pointed at the last sentence.

"The you-know-what."

"There was something about it in the space exhibit, too," Nick said. "It must be related to space-based solar power. Like what Mom and Dad have been working on."

Tesla nodded grimly.

"We know someone's after their project, whatever it is. I think someone's trying to get their hands on this Solanow thingie, too."

Two large, feathery figures loomed behind Nick and Tesla. "When the Hall of Genius went haywire this afternoon, it overloaded the power for the whole museum," said Uncle Newt. "Everything went down—*including the security system*."

"They're not out to sabotage the Hall of Genius after all," said Carstairs. "They're planning to rob one of the exhibits!"

Silas finally joined the others by the Nikola Tesla display.

"All that from reading one sign? Wow. I'm going to have to start paying more attention to those things." He looked at Tesla, his expression turning hopeful. "So does that mean you know who's got

DeMarco?"

"That's obvious now," Tesla said.

"Oh, come on!" Silas cried. "*What's* obvious?"

"The problem is, we still don't have any proof," said Nick. "How do we stop them?"

Unfortunately for Silas, the conversation was moving along without him.

"Reverse that and you might have our answer," Uncle Newt was saying to Nick.

"Uh, how do we stop them? The problem is, we still don't have any proof," Nick said.

Uncle Newt shook his head.

"Maybe we could get our proof by *not* stopping them."

Nick, Tesla, Carstairs, and Silas all looked confused.

"Ah!" Tesla said after a moment.

"Oh!" said Nick a moment after that.

"I like it!" said Carstairs a moment after that.

"Tesla and I came up with an idea a few weeks ago that we could reuse now with just a couple modifications," Nick said. "It's a—"

"Semi-invisible fluorescent ink tracker," said Tesla, already heading for her uncle's toolbox. "I'm on it!"

"I still don't understand!" Silas wailed. Then: "Oooooh! I get it."

Did he really get it? By then, everyone was too busy to ask.

SUPER-CYBORG GADGET GLOVE

FINGER #4 (PINKY): NICK AND TESLA'S SEMI-INVISIBLE BAD GUY TRACKER AND SECRET MESSAGE MIXTURE

THE STUFF

- Your gadget glove

- 1 5-mm High-Brightness Ultraviolet LED (Radio Shack item #3107633)

- 1 CR2032 3-volt button battery (Radio Shack item #2102855)

- Small bowl or cup

- Water

- Highlighter marker

- A finger's length of 24-gauge solid speaker wire

- Hot-glue gun

- Scissors

- Wire strippers

- Electrical tape

- Highlighter marker

- Cotton swab

Note: Nick and Tesla are going to [SPOILER ALERT] spill their secret message mixture on the floor, but you should NOT do that! You could ruin the floor or carpeting, which will make your parents mad and could put an end to your adventures for quite a while. Instead, make the message mixture in small batches and use it to write secret notes that only the wearer of the gadget glove can read.

THE SETUP

1. Wire the ultraviolet LED and battery to the pinky of the glove the same way that you wired the Nick Signal to the index finger (see page 65). The positive (long) LED wire should connect to the pinky wire, and the negative (short) LED wire should connect to the negative side of the battery. Another wire should connect the positive side of the battery to the thumb wire.

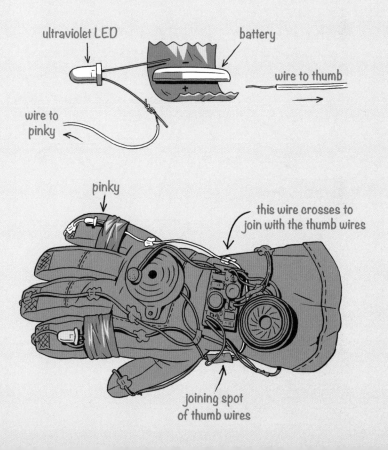

ultraviolet LED

battery

wire to thumb

wire to pinky

pinky

this wire crosses to join with the thumb wires

joining spot of thumb wires

2. Pour 2 teaspoons (10 ml) of water into the small bowl. Dip the highlighter in the water and hold it there until the water turns yellow.

THE FINAL STEPS

1. Dip the cotton swab into the mixture and use it to write a message. Let dry. If the message is too visible, add some water to the mixture and write a new message.

2. Bring together the exposed wires on the thumb and pinky to activate the ultraviolet LED. Shine the light on the message to make it visible!

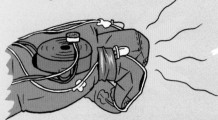

14

It was Silas's idea to use the glove again.

"You guys are making another doohickey?" he said to Nick and Tesla. They were pulling markers from the toolbox while Uncle Newt and Carstairs removed an ultraviolet LED from a box of fake plutonium in the Robert Oppenheimer display. "You should stick it on Glovey. It's all set with batteries and wires and stuff. Plus, it'll add to my awesome powers!"

"We'd just be adding a teeny little ultraviolet light," Tesla said.

"Exactly." Silas clenched his

fists and stared off into the distance. "Now Laser-hand shall be invincible!"

Tesla didn't point out that Glovey didn't really belong to Silas (or that a UV light would hardly make someone invincible). She just hurried off to get the gadget glove.

Silas might have been losing his mind, but a good idea is a good idea.

"Be right back!" Tesla shouted.

"You'd better be!" her brother yelled after her.

For once, Tesla didn't get lost as she ran through the museum's back corridors. She usually worked best under pressure, and there was plenty of pressure now. They had to be ready by the time Ms. Mavis led her party guests into the Hall of Genius or else they'd miss their chance to catch the bad guys in the act—and never find out what they'd done with DeMarco.

Hiroko was alone in the security office when Tesla came in.

"Where's Berg?" Tesla asked.

"He left fifteen minutes ago," Hiroko said. "He went on and on about how many pounds he can bench press and his all-protein diet, and then he looked at the clock and said something about it being 'show time' and took off. Any sign of the police?"

"They're not coming."

"*What?*"

"I'll explain on the way to the Hall of Genius," Tesla said. She pointed at the gadget glove spread out on the desk nearby. "And don't forget to bring that."

When Tesla and Hiroko popped through the hidden door behind Einstein's blackboard, they found Carstairs and Uncle Newt consulting over the little UV bulb while Nick pulled the dye packs out of the markers. (Uncle Newt had changed back into his normal clothes, but for some reason Carstairs left on his owl costume, leaving him looking like a man-bird from the neck down.) Silas was at the far end of the Hall of Genius, gazing out at the gala.

"Glovey!" he said, taking a step toward Hiroko.

"What's Ms. Mavis up to now?" Nick barked at him.

Crestfallen, Silas turned away and looked back out into the atrium.

"She's still thanking donors," he said. "I think she's going to wrap it up soon, though. The crowd's starting to get pretty antsy."

"Keep an eye on 'em!" Nick ordered. He turned to his sister and lowered his voice. "I thought I should keep him away from Glovey. I didn't want him to try to grab it and—"

"Gimme!" Uncle Newt said, grabbing the gadget glove from Hiroko.

"Well, hello to you, too!" Hiroko groused.

"Sorry! No time for pleasantries! Emergency! Alacrity! Fast, fast, fast!"

Uncle Newt rushed over to his toolbox and immediately began tinkering with the glove. Tesla, Carstairs, and Hiroko crowded around to peer over his shoulders, taking turns annoying him with suggestions and corrections as he hurriedly hooked up the ultraviolet LED to a battery and attached them to the glove. Nick, meanwhile, started squeezing ink from the highligher markers into some water-filled plastic bags. (He'd retrieved the bags from the garbage can in the staff lunchroom while his sister was off getting the glove.)

"Ms. Mavis is finally done talking," Silas reported after a few minutes.

"She's leading everybody into the *Something NEW*

under the Sun exhibit," he said a couple minutes after that.

"I hear a lot of oohing and ahhhing," he said a couple more minutes after that.

"Now there's applause," he said a minute after that.

"They're all coming out again," he said less than a minute after that.

"Ms. Mavis is leading them this way," he said thirty seconds after that.

"She's past the dinosaurs," he said twenty seconds after that.

"She's almost to the big brain," he said ten seconds after that.

"They're here!" he said five seconds after that.

And he was running away from the entrance when he said it.

"Good," Uncle Newt said. "I'm done."

Tesla snatched up the gadget glove, Nick grabbed the plastic bags, and they both started herding Silas and Carstairs toward the back exit.

"Go, go, go!" Tesla barked.

And off they went, went, went.

"Oh. What a pleasant surprise," Katherine Mavis

said a moment later as she led the crowd into the exhibit. For a split second, the look on her face made it plain the surprise wasn't really pleasant at all. "Here we have two of the geniuses behind our Hall of Genius—Dr. Newton Holt and Dr. Hiroko Sakurai. Uh, is everything ready?"

Uncle Newt smiled.

"I guess we're about to find out."

Nick, Tesla, Silas, and Carstairs weaved their way through the corridors until they reached the side service entrance to the museum's atrium. It was the same spot from which the kids and Uncle Newt had first spied on the reopening gala, only now the lobby was nearly deserted. All the guests had crowded into the Hall of Genius. The only people left in sight were waiters gathering up abandoned plates and glasses and two of the Coolicious McBrainys, one tall and one small, trying to entertain a bored-looking bartender with some extremely sloppy breakdancing. And, on the far side of the lobby, two guards stationed outside the *Something NEW under the Sun* exhibit.

Tesla nodded at the guards—and the entrance just beyond them.

"There's the target," she said. "We've got to get closer so we're ready when the moment comes."

Nick handed her one of the water-filled bags and then gave another to Silas.

"You'd better wait here," he said to Carstairs. He looked down at the man's feather-covered body. "You'd probably be a bit conspicuous."

"Sorry. I'd be conspicuous if I took the costume off, too. My clothes are soaked," Carstairs said sheepishly. "Be careful out there."

"Don't worry," Silas said. He reached out to take the gadget glove from Tesla. "Nobody's going to mess with us while I've got—hey!"

Before Silas could get the glove, Tesla had given it to Nick.

Silas was great for sitting on people, but for what lay ahead she trusted her brother more.

"Sorry, Silas. We did another round of rock, paper, scissors while you were on lookout duty," she lied. "I played for you and lost."

"Awww! What did you start with?"

NICK AND TESLA'S SUPER-CYBORG GADGET GLOVE

"Uh, um . . . paper."

"Well, that was your mistake right there!" Silas cried. "Rock! Always start with rock!"

Silas watched miserably as Nick pulled on the glove and tested the new UV light.

The LED lit up with a pale purple glow.

"All right," Nick said. He knew this was the moment when his sister would usually say something bold and rousing like "Let's do this thing" or "Time to catch some bad guys." But all he could think of was "Let's go get DeMarco," so that's what he said.

And that was enough. Tesla and Silas nodded, and together the three of them started walking toward the *Something NEW under the Sun* exhibit. They tried to look nonchalant as they crossed the atrium, but that turned out to be hard to do when you're walking fast with a bag of ink-stained water clutched behind your back.

Tesla gazed in mock wonder at the dinosaurs.

Nick pretended to appreciate the museum's architecture.

Silas started whistling.

"Stop it," Tesla hissed.

"We're trying not to be noticed, Silas," Nick

grated out.

"Okay, geez, sorry," Silas grumbled. "Maybe if I was wearing Glovey I wouldn't be so nervous."

He threw Nick a hopeful look.

Nick went back to admiring the architecture.

"Oh, great," Tesla muttered a moment later.

"What?" said Nick.

"Check out the guy on the right."

They were close enough to the guards now to see their faces. And their muscles. Which, in one guard's case, were so big and bulging that they looked like a bunch of watermelons stuffed into a blue uniform.

"Berg," Nick sighed. "What do you think he'll do when he notices us?"

But before Tesla could give Nick an answer, Berg did.

"Hey," he said, turning their way with a scowl. "What are you still doing here? The party's for invited guests and Learnasium employees only."

"Well . . . ," Tesla said.

And that was as far as she got.

A cacophonous chorus of shrill, screeching voices burst from the Hall of Genius, followed seconds later by the sound of screaming and stampeding feet. There was a distant crash of breaking glass and the whirr and clatter of machinery running so fast that it was starting to fly apart. Every light in the museum began to flicker.

"It's happening again," Tesla said. "Just like we thought it would."

Nick nodded. "Robo-geddon, round 2. Right on schedule."

"Cool!" said Silas.

Elegant partygoers in tuxes and gowns began streaming out of the Hall of Genius, shrieking.

"Something's going on over there!" Berg noted astutely.

Two guards ran out of the *Something NEW* exhibit. "What's happening?" one of them asked Berg.

"That!" Berg said, pointing at the frantic crowd across the atrium. "Come on!"

All four guards ran off toward the Hall of Genius.

Before they were even halfway there, the lights went out completely, plunging the entire museum into utter darkness.

The racket kicked up by the Hall of Genius's haywire animatronics instantly ended, but the screams grew louder, and there was a thud and a grunted

"Oof!"

"I think I just ran into a dinosaur," Berg groaned.

Silas started to laugh.

Nick and Tesla shushed him.

"Listen," Nick whispered.

A familiar swishing sound was growing louder. Closer. Then it began to fade away.

"Now," Tesla said.

She brought around her bag of inky water and hurled it at the entrance to the solar power exhibit. Or at least she *hoped* she was hurling it toward the exhibit. It was impossible to tell how accurate her aim was in the dark. But she'd lined up her shot before the lights went out, and she heard it go *splat* in what sounded like the right spot. A few seconds later there were two more *splooshes*—Nick's and Silas's bags bursting nearby.

After that, they heard no sound except for a few panicked cries and shouts, and then another loud "Oof!" from Berg. Then the *sw-sw-swishing* returned, growing louder before quickly fading away.

And the lights came back on.

"Ow!" said absolutely everybody in the museum, simultaneously pressing their hands to their faces to block the sudden light.

After some rubbing and blinking, everyone's eyes readjusted.

And that's when the complaining started.

"I've never been so frightened in my life!" a woman said.

"Einstein's head hit me right in the face!" said a man.

"That was Charles Darwin," someone pointed out.

"Whatever! I didn't come here to play dodge ball with a bunch of body parts!" the man shot back.

"We should sue!" said about a dozen people to their spouses.

"I told you this would happen," said Ellen Wharton-Wheeler. The tall, stern curator was standing next to an ashen-faced Katherine Mavis. "You turned my museum into a funhouse, and now it's ruined."

The two women were just outside the Hall of Genius. Mojo Jones and Ruffin, the museum's rumpled chief of security, stood beside them, both looking like they knew they should be doing something but were too stunned to figure out what.

Katherine Mavis cleared her throat and pasted a

thin, tremulous smile onto her face.

"That's what they call 'technical difficulties,' friends!" she said cheerily to the unhappy mob around her. "Just one of the little setbacks you have to expect when you're as extreme as the X-Treme Learnasium! Let's take a minute to catch our breath and then we can continue the tour with our new space exhibit. I can assure you, there won't be any more surprises like *that!*" But before she could continue trying to calm the crowd, a new voice interrupted her.

"Ladies and gentlemen: your attention, please!" the voice boomed. "A young man may be in danger, and if we're going to help him, then everyone needs to stay exactly where they are!"

It was Tesla. She'd climbed atop the giant brain near the Hall of Genius and was standing on it, looking down at the crowd with her arms outstretched.

"Hey! Get offa that!" Ruffin barked at her.

"I will in just a minute, sir. But first I have some work for you. If you want to check on whatever you've got on loan from Solanow over there"—Tesla waggled her thumb at the *Something NEW under the Sun* exhibit—"I think you'll find that it's gone."

Ruffin rolled his eyes. "You still think there's some kind of supervillain running around here plotting and kidnapping people?"

"Yes," Tesla said. "What just happened in the Hall of Genius was no accident. It was a diversion. And it worked."

Tesla turned to look pointedly at Berg and the other security guards, who'd been slowly creeping toward the brain with the obvious intention of pulling her off of it.

Ruffin's eyes widened when he saw them.

"What are you doing over here?" he snapped.

"Well, there was all the screaming and the yelling and stuff," Berg said. "And now there's a kid standing on our brain."

"So who's watching the microwave transmitter and the rectenna?" Ruffin asked.

Berg looked around at the other guards. The other guards looked back at Berg.

"Oh. Uh, nobody, I guess."

"Get back there, you—!"

Then Ruffin suddenly seemed to remember that he was being watched by a few hundred well-dressed spectators. He swallowed whatever word was going to follow "you" and lowered his voice.

"Please be so good as to check the exhibit for me, Donald," he said instead.

"You got it, Chief!"

Berg saluted and lumbered off as quickly as his thick, squat legs could carry him.

"Watch out for the water!" Tesla called after him.

Berg ignored her.

"What water?" Ruffin asked.

"Whoa!" Berg hollered as he went slipping and sliding through the puddle in front of the solar power exhibit.

"That water," Tesla said. "It's got fluorescent ink in it."

"Florescent ink?"

"This day just gets weirder and weirder," Mojo Jones said, putting a hand to his head.

"Will someone please tell me why we're standing around listening to a fifth grader?" Wharton-Wheeler sneered.

"Seventh grader, in the fall," Tesla told her coldly. "And here comes your answer."

Berg came pounding back out of the solar power exhibit.

"The—!" he started to say.

And then he went skidding through the puddle again, only managing to remain upright thanks to a vigorous flapping of his overdeveloped arms.

"The kid's right!" he said once he'd regained his balance. "The equipment from Solanow—it's gone!"

A gasp rose from the crowd.

Ruffin looked like he was about to explode. Mavis looked like she was about to faint.

"Don't worry," Tesla told them. "The thieves didn't get far."

"How do you know?" Mavis asked, her voice hoarse, her eyes hollow.

"Because they're right here," Nick said.

He was approaching the Hall of Genius hunched over, with his right hand pointed down. The UV LED on the gadget glove was shining, lighting up tracks that glowed a ghostly purple-blue on the smooth museum floor.

Silas followed a few steps behind him, looking profoundly jealous.

"The ink was so that we could follow whoever went into that exhibit when the lights went out," Nick said. "The trail leads here, though I think that's probably obvious by now."

Aglow on the ground were two sets of footprints.

Big, clunky footprints, which split in front into three sharp points.

The footprints of oversized birds.

Nick stopped in front of the two Coolicious Mc-Brainys, one towering, one tiny, who were standing together at the edge of the crowd. Their feathery bellies seemed more swollen than before, as if each one was about to lay a big batch of eggs.

"Who?" the bigger owl hooted. "Us?"

"Yeah," Nick said. "You."

The Cooliciouses looked at each other and then spun on their taloned heels and took off running.

"Stop those owls!" Nick cried as the Coolicious McBrainys tried to scamper away across the atrium.

The museum's V.I.P. guests seemed too hypnotized by the bizarre scenario to do anything. They'd come to eat appetizers and hobnob, not to chase runaway mascots.

Silas, on the other hand, was ready to leap into action.

"Oh, yeah!" he bellowed. "Time for me to do my thing!"

He took off after the owls and threw himself onto the taller one's back. The owl just kept running with Silas draped over his shoulders like a backpack.

Then Berg flew in from the side and flung himself on both of them.

"Gently!" Tesla yelled at him. "They've still got the thingamajig and the whatchamacallit!"

"You heard the young lady!" Ruffin yelled. "Gently!"

By now the other guards had joined the chase, and they quickly caught up to the smaller Coolicious, latched on, and smoothly but firmly turned the bird around.

Berg, meanwhile, had managed to twist one of the giant Cooliciouses's wings behind its broad back.

"Give it up, punk, or you'll never fly again," he snarled.

"Ha! Good one!" said Silas, who'd slid off the owl's back and was now wrapped around its waist.

The big Coolicious finally stopped trying to run away.

"All right, all right!" it squawked. "Not so hard! That hurts!"

Berg (with unnecessary but eager help from Silas) marched the owl back to the middle of the atrium to stand, sullen and slump shouldered, beside the other smaller Coolicious.

"Unzip their outfits, and I think you'll find what you're looking for," Nick said.

The guards looked at Ruffin.

"You might as well do what he says," he told them. "These kids are on a roll."

The guards leaned in close to the owls, hunting through their dark feathers until they found the zippers hidden beneath their beaks.

There was a ziiiiiiip, then another, and suddenly it was obvious why the Coolicious costumes were bulging so much at the belly.

Stuffed inside each suit was a bulky piece of equipment. One had a short row of black panels attached to a jutting cylinder the size of a can of tennis balls. The other was a single broad, flat, plastic board with a cable running out the back that ended in a plain, old-fashioned electrical plug.

"Eww," Berg said, grimacing, as he pulled the board out of the big Coolicious's suit. "It's all slimy."

"Hey, it's hot in here," the owl whined.

"So that one draws energy from light and beams it out as microwaves," Tesla guessed, pointing at the piece of equipment being taken from the little

Coolicious's outfit. "And the other one converts the microwaves into electricity."

Katherine Mavis nodded, looking impressed. "It's cutting-edge technology. Solanow loaned us those prototypes as a promotional venture," she said. "In the exhibit, we use a heat lamp to power a lava lamp from across the room."

Tesla must not have looked impressed, because a moment later the curator added, "A really big lava lamp."

"It looks cooler than it sounds!" someone from the crowd threw in.

"How is it that you know so much about wireless power transfer?" Ellen Wharton-Wheeler asked Tesla suspiciously.

She shrugged. "Hey, my name is Tesla," she said.

"What I want to know is who these two are," Ruffin said with a jerk of the head at the captive Cooliciouses. The guards were still gripping them by the wings.

"Why not take a look?" Nick suggested.

Ruffin laughed in a weary, resigned sort of way. "Why not, indeed," he said. He turned toward the guards. "Gentlemen, if you would."

"Off with their heads!" Silas cackled as Berg and another guard took hold of the big round owl masks and whipped them away.

The short Coolicious turned out to be a scowling twenty-something woman with a bald head, pierced nostrils, and tattoos covering half her face.

The tall Coolicious was a man with a long mournful face and dark hair buzzed short into a flattop.

They were both wearing heavy gray goggles.

"What's with the weird glasses?" Berg asked.

"Night-vision goggles," Tesla said. "So they'd be able to see after the lights went out." She turned to her brother. "Looks like we were right about the mastermind."

"Mastermind?" the bald woman snorted. "Yeah, right."

"Who are you talking about?" the director demanded.

"The controls for the Hall of Genius had been hacked. The phone system, too," Tesla said. "We figured there was only one person with the technical know-how to do all that. And now we have proof."

Nick pointed at the prisoners.

"Don't they look familiar?"

Mavis squinted at the man and the woman. Ruffin and Wharton-Wheeler and nearly everyone in the crowd did, too.

"Now that you mention it, I do feel like I've seen them before somewhere," Mavis said.

"You have," said Nick, and he pulled a small flat rectangle from his pocket and walked it over to her.

"No," she gasped when he handed it to her.

She was looking down at the picture on a Migraine Monkey Missile Test refrigerator magnet.

The Cooliciouses were two-thirds of the band.

Mavis whirled around to face the band's front man: the museum's senior system manager, Mojo Jones.

"Mojo! How could you? I onboard you into the most impactful project on my TDL, and you calamatize everything?"

"What? Me? I haven't calma—calmata—I haven't done anything!" Mojo said, blinking wide, innocent eyes. "Honestly, Katherine, I'm as shocked by all this as you."

"Oh, give it up, Mojo," the little tattooed woman snapped. "I'll tell you how he could do it, lady. Someone offered him $100,000 to sneak those power gizmos out of the museum, that's how."

"Be quiet, Pauline," the tall man whispered to her.

"He said he was gonna use the money to shoot a video for one of our songs," she continued.

"Don't talk till we have lawyers, Pauline," the tall man muttered.

"Hey, Mojo. I've been meaning to tell you," Pauline went on. "Your rapping stinks."

"Oh, yeah?" Jones spat back. "I'd have thought you were too busy messing up all the bass lines to notice!"

"Pauline is a great bassist!" the big guy protested.

Mojo rolled his eyes.

"Says the drummer with no sense of rhythm."

"Hey!" Silas roared, stepping in between Mojo and his squabbling band mates. "Just shut up and tell us where our friend is!"

"Well, which is it?" said the tall man. "Do you want us to shut up or do you want us to tell you—ow!"

Pauline had stomped on his foot.

"We put him in one of the storage rooms," she told Silas. "Number 31. We were gonna let him go on the way out, I swear."

"Come on!" Tesla said.

She ran from the atrium, with Nick and Silas close behind her.

Pauline watched them go, and then she stomped on the tall man's foot again.

"I told you we should've quit the band," she said.

Uncle Newt and Hiroko caught up with the kids as

once again they sprinted through the museum corridors.

"We saw the whole thing!" Uncle Newt panted. "Wow! I mean . . . just . . . wow!"

"Nice going!" Hiroko said.

"We're not done yet," Tesla said.

"This way!" said Nick, taking a sharp left.

Seconds later, they were at a door with STORAGE 31 stenciled on it. It wasn't locked, and when they burst through they found themselves in a room filled with huge red and gray coils of foam and boulder-sized chunks of what looked like half-chewed pizza. A sign leaning against one wall read GOING WITH YOUR GUT: A JOURNEY THROUGH THE DIGESTIVE SYSTEM.

"These must be leftovers from one of the museum's old exhibits," Nick said.

"But where's DeMarco?" said Silas.

Muffled grunts erupted from one corner of the room. They followed the sound to what was either a giant bladder or the world's largest sculpture of a lima bean.

Behind it, they found DeMarco tied to a chair and gagged with a Migraine Monkey Missile Test bandana.

The first words out of his mouth when Tesla untied the bandana were "It's about time!"

The second words were "What'd I miss?"

" . . . and then we found you behind the giant lima bean," Silas said once he'd finished his highly edited (and not entirely accurate) overview of the past hour's events. "What happened to *you?*"

"I got captured," DeMarco said with a nonchalant shrug, as if this was something that happened to him every other day.

"I think there's a little more to it than that," Tesla said.

"Not really. Getting captured is pretty boring. I've just been sitting in here for, like, ever. I knew they weren't gonna hurt me—that bald girl, Pauline, kept apologizing and telling Mojo and the other guy they were idiots. So all I could do was wait and wait and wait. I'm just glad I didn't have to go to the bathroom. That would've been awful!"

"What about *before* you got captured, DeMarco?"

Nick prompted.

"Oh. That. It was pretty boring, too. That meeting I was supposed to record? The one where Ms. Mavis and Ms. Wharton-Wheeler—"

"Wharton-Wheeler," Tesla corrected him.

"That's what I said."

"Oh, right. Sorry."

"Anyway, that meeting where they were going to reveal their evil plot against the Learnasium? A total waste of time."

"You're kidding," said Nick.

"Nope. See, Ms. Wharton-Wheeler wrote 'destroying the museum from within' because that's what she thought Ms. Mavis was doing. You know, by changing the name of the place and turning it into an 'amusement park.'" DeMarco stretched out his arms as he talked. "Sure feels good to move! Anyway, their whole conversation was all this junk about marketing and 'rebranding' and how to 'position' the museum with donors. Lucky for me, Ms. Mavis cut the meeting short to go get ready for the big party. Five more minutes of listening to that boring stuff and I would've jumped out from under the table and run out of the room screaming."

"So how'd you get captured?" Tesla asked him.

DeMarco jogged in place for a few seconds. "Whew, my legs were cramping up. So I waited for the two of them to leave and then I slipped out and headed back to the Hall of Genius. But, well, I took a little detour."

"You got lost," Tesla said.

DeMarco ignored her and kept talking. "I guess Mojo Jones wasn't expecting anyone to be in this part of the museum today, because I came around a corner and there he was, telling two people in Coolicious McBrainy suits where to hide when the lights go out tonight. I turned right around and tried to get out of there, but they caught up to me."

"But you used the glove to record a message for us first," Nick said.

DeMarco grinned. "Yup. I tossed it around a corner where they wouldn't see it. Pretty brilliant, huh?"

"It would've helped a bit if you'd said who was chasing you," Tesla pointed out.

DeMarco's grin faded. "Hey, I didn't *know* I was about to get grabbed and tied up in a storage room! Geez, Tez, sometimes you can be so—"

"I'm sorry, DeMarco. All that stuff wouldn't have

happened if I hadn't pushed everybody into investigating the sabotage."

"Ah, forget it," DeMarco answered. He smiled again, rolling his head from side to side to loosen his stiff neck muscles. "You know, compared to some of the stuff my sisters have put me through, having to sit in a chair for a few hours was no big deal."

At that moment, a small herd of adults came charging in to the storeroom. Uncle Newt and Hiroko, who had gone to find the authorities once they saw that DeMarco was okay, were in the lead, followed by Ruffin, Wharton-Wheeler, and Carstairs (who was still dressed as an owl with a man's head). They made DeMarco run through what had happened to him all over again, though this time he left out any reference to the meeting he'd been trying to eavesdrop on. He just said he'd gotten lost in the hallways when he ran into Mojo and the other Migraine Monkeys.

"I'm very, very sorry you had that experience in our museum, son," Ruffin said when DeMarco was done.

"Don't worry about it," DeMarco told him. "It was something new."

"I'm sorry the museum's reopening was ruined," Tesla said. "I wish we could have found a way to avoid that."

To Tesla's surprise, Ruffin laughed.

"The reopening hasn't been ruined at all," he said. "Most of our guests think they just witnessed the most 'x-treme' publicity stunt ever. I mean, it's perfect, isn't it? A bunch of kids use science to foil a heist in the Learnasium? If you go back out to the party, you'll probably get a standing ovation."

"And you'd deserve it," Ellen Wharton-Wheeler said. "What you did tonight was extraordinary. Young people like you are what this museum is supposed to be all about." She offered the kids a small, uncertain smile. "I'm sorry if I seemed to have forgotten that today."

Nick and Tesla smiled back at her.

"We understand," Tesla said.

"You were under a lot of stress," said Nick.

"You could always make it up to us by letting me have this," said Silas.

He patted the giant foam-rubber hot dog he'd been sitting on.

"I don't think I could do that," she said. "But I

would like all of your help with a new exhibit you've inspired." She looked at the gadget glove on Nick's hand. "I'm thinking we could call it *Building a Cooler You: A Cyborg Workshop*. Or something like that."

"I love it!" Silas said. He turned to stare at the gadget glove, too. "Speaking of which—you don't need that anymore, do you, Nick?"

Without a word, Nick stripped off the gadget glove and handed it to his friend.

"Glovey!" Silas cried, giving the glove a hug.

"Glovey?" said Wharton-Wheeler. She looked as if she was already having second thoughts about a cyborg workshop.

"You know, I think this glove needs only one more thing to be perfect," an oblivious Silas said as he pulled the glove onto his hand. "A web shooter!"

"We'll get on that tomorrow," Tesla said sarcastically.

"I'm afraid you won't be able to work in our lab at home tomorrow," Uncle Newt said to her. "You'll be spending the day with Silas's family again, assuming they can take you. Hiroko and I will need to be back at the museum bright and early to repair the Hall of Genius."

"Again," Hiroko grumbled.

"But we'll have expert help this time!" Uncle Newt said. He turned to Carstairs. "I'll get Katherine Mavis to rehire you, Mark. Now it's obvious that the problems with the exhibit weren't your fault, and we'll need your help to root out whatever bugs Mojo Jones programmed into the controls."

"Thanks, Newt," Carstairs said. "I'd like that."

"Hurrah," Nick said through a stifled yawn. "A happy ending. Can we go home now?"

Ruffin shook his head.

"Sorry, not yet. We finally got a call through to the real police. They'll need statements from all of you."

"Oh, man, that'll take forever. I was supposed to be home already," DeMarco said with a groan. "What am I going to say to my mom and dad?"

For the first time that day, he looked as if he was capable of feeling fear.

Silas, meanwhile, hadn't even heard what Ruffin said. He was too busy turning the lights on the gadget glove on and off while making *p-shew p-shew* noises.

Nick just yawned again and trudged off to a giant hamburger in the corner. When he reached it, he climbed on top and curled up in a ball.

The grownups launched into a conversation about Mojo Jones and his accomplices and what charges they were likely to face. ("Is unauthorized use of an owl costume illegal?" wondered Uncle Newt aloud. "If so, we might be in trouble, Mark.")

Meanwhile, Tesla walked over to her brother.

"You okay?"

Nick sighed heavily.

"All the running around and uncovering and confronting and unmasking . . . it wipes me out."

"Not me," said Tesla. "I could really go for some pizza."

Nick lifted his head just high enough to give his sister a look.

"You eat this stuff up," he said. "Literally."

He dropped his head back onto the hamburger and closed his eyes.

"Funny that somebody was after Solanow's wireless power equipment," Tesla mused as if her brother hadn't spoken at all. "Just like someone's after whatever Mom and Dad have been working on."

"Tesla . . . ," Nick said.

"I know, I know. You think I'm seeing conspiracies and mysteries everywhere these days. But haven't I always been right?"

"Tez . . ."

"I wonder if there's a link between Solanow and Mom and Dad's work for the government. We'll have to figure that out somehow. Not that I'm looking for more mysteries or trouble. I'm just curious—and I know you are, too."

Tesla went on for a while, talking about how she and her brother could dig up background information on Solanow via their uncle and Katherine Mavis and the Internet. Nick didn't interrupt.

He was too busy snoring.

About the Authors

"SCIENCE BOB" PFLUGFELDER is an award-winning elementary school science teacher. His fun and informative approach to science has led to television appearances on the History Channel and Access Hollywood. He is also a regular guest on *Jimmy Kimmel Live*, *The Dr. Oz Show*, and *Live with Kelly & Michael*. Articles on Bob's experiments have appeared in *People*, *Nickelodeon* magazine, *Popular Science*, *Disney's Family Fun*, and *Wired*. He lives in Watertown, Massachusetts.

STEVE HOCKENSMITH is the author of the Edgar-nominated Holmes on the Range mystery series. His other books include the New York Times best seller *Pride and Prejudice and Zombies: Dawn of the Dreadfuls* and the short-story collection *Naughty: Nine Tales of Christmas Crime*. He lives with his wife and two children about forty minutes from Half Moon Bay, California.

Collect all of the electrifying
Nick and Tesla adventures!

Nick and Tesla's
High-Voltage Danger Lab

Nick and Tesla's
Robot Army Rampage

Nick and Tesla's
Secret Agent Gadget Battle

Nick and Tesla's
Super-Cyborg Gadget Glove

Visit NickandTesla.com for updates, instructions, photos, and more!